WHITE BOYS
and RIVER GIRLS

WHITE BOYS
and RIVER GIRLS

STORIES BY

PAULA K. GOVER

ALGONQUIN BOOKS OF CHAPEL HILL • 1995

Published by
ALGONQUIN BOOKS OF CHAPEL HILL
Post Office Box 2225
Chapel Hill, North Carolina 27515-2225

a division of
WORKMAN PUBLISHING COMPANY, INC.
708 Broadway
New York, New York 10003

This is a work of fiction. Names, characters, places, and incidents are either the product of the author's imagination or are used fictitiously. Any resemblance to actual events or locales or persons, living or dead, is entirely coincidental.

Library of Congress Cataloging-in-Publication Data
Gover, Paula K., 1955–
    White boys and river girls : stories / Paula K. Gover.—1st ed.
        p.   cm.
    Contents: White boys and river girls—My naked beauty—Bastard child—A woman like me—Necessary distance—Black boy in a white girl's world—The kid's been called nigger before—Mistress of cats—Chances with Johnson.
    ISBN 1–56512–049–3
    1. Women—Southern States—Social life and customs—Fiction.
I. Title.
PS3557.O919W45   1995
813'.54—dc20   94–40901
                                                              CIP

10 9 8 7 6 5 4 3 2 1
First Edition

Grateful acknowledgment is made to *The Virginia Quarterly Review*, *Ms.*, *College Times*, *Story*, *Southern Review*, *Crosscurrents*, and *New Stories from the South, 1993*, where some of the stories first appeared in earlier versions.

For my son Aaron David, the music of my dreams, and in memory of my father, who loved my son without measure.

and

To S., my first kiss. Always.

CONTENTS

What is most beautiful in virile men is something feminine; what is most beautiful in feminine women is something masculine.

—Susan Sontag, *Against Interpretation* (1961)

I've been things and seen places.

—Mae West, *I'm No Angel* (1933 film)

WHITE BOYS
AND RIVER GIRLS

Yolanda Jean Louisell was waiting tables at the Tenderloin Ballroom that summer we collided, working five or six nights a week for Willie B. Lamb. The Tenderloin sits a good mile north of feeling like a part of Savannah, facing the river at the end of a tired-looking stretch of fish shops and boatyards what follow on down the coast. While I'd become one of Willie B.'s regulars when he hired up Yolanda, I could tell right off that she wasn't my regular type. She was the kind I sometimes picked up with in between the tall, blond cool-drink-for-the-eyes numbers I prefer, the kind what don't give you nothing to think about much, except for the smell of their hair. Not that Yolanda wasn't a looker in her own rights—small, dark-eyed, skin so pale, like she never seen daylight or breathed in air. The kind with "Slow down, Donnie-boy, watch the road now" written clean across her face. No. She wasn't my regular type.

Take Cynthia, for instance. That's who I'm hanging out with these days. Three inches under my six foot two, small white wedges of skin at her breasts and hips when she peels off her bikini, eyes green as kiwis. She's working on a portfolio for a modeling agency out of Savannah. Hopes to make it into videos with the house band from the Tenderloin. And she might. Her brother Marvin works lights for the band, and he knows someone who knows someone who could maybe help now that the band's got a recording contract. She's from Tyler, like me, and says she remembers me from when I played football, but she's just enough younger so it's okay I don't remember her. And she's slimmed down since back then, though I don't say nothing about that. Only, I know how she fusses about the pale stretch marks on her bottom and radiating out like a star-burst from her nipples, but they're not visible to no one but me. Or so she says.

Last weekend Cynthia worked a car show in Macon, stretching all five foot eleven inches of her attributes across machine-waxed hoods and bumpers and quarter panels. She's got the glossies developed already and tucked into her portfolio, just so. She takes great pains in arranging them in special order, holding them up under the light in the dining el, the tips of her nails at the corners, going, "What do you think, Donnie, this one or this? Which first? Which one is the real me?" Course, aren't none of them the real her, not the Cynthia I see each morning, sheet wrinkles on her cheeks and sour-breathed as she rolls against me in our bed. But then, what do I know? So I tell her this one or that, point at the photos, smile, say they're all real nice, and that's what she likes to hear.

When the guys come around after work, I kind of flip through the portfolio, looking from the television set to their faces, acting indifferent about how they go to looking from Cynthia in the flesh at the dining-room table, clipping coupons, with hair tied back, then their heads bobbing back over the pages again. I go, "She's got it all right," watching them react to Cynthia's body all oiled and tanned and spread out in the photos, tucked inside those bikinis what weren't never meant for swimming.

Cynthia's big dream is a condo on the coast—full basement, white shutters, privacy fence, the whole shot. We drive around Sundays after church and stop at the open-house signs near the beach, going twenty miles in either direction from the city. She says commuting is stylish these days. We walk up the narrow white sidewalks to the display models, real proper, like we was married or something, me in a clean shirt for once, her all wobbly on heels in her church clothes, and only I know she's not wearing any panties.

Cynthia and I got this two-bedroom apartment in Garden City off Highway 21. It's cheap because the airport's right there back of the place, and to be honest, our neighbors are mostly poor working people, but I kind of like that, you know. Feels like I'm where I belong, even if somebody's fighting brings the law out every week or so. But when someone asks Cynthia where we stay, she smiles and tells them, "In the city," slow-voiced and lying so pretty they believe it, and I don't understand that, but women are like that, ask anyone.

It doesn't take much to keep Cynthia happy, just keep saying how god-awful nice she looks and act like I can't think of nothing all day but getting home to her body all stretched out in the chaise lounge next to the pool by the rental office with a puddle of baby oil in her navel. She's easy to live with because most of the time she's too busy working on herself to know I'm around, sticking little foam pads between her toes and fingers, painting her nails while watching the television, flipping between Geraldo and soaps and music videos, studying who she wants to be, shaking bottles of polish so the little beads go clicking around. She spends two hours a day on the exercise bike in our living room, and when she's not busy puffing away there, working the handlebar levers in a criss-cross, increasing the resistance on the wheel, she goes into the kitchen and runs carrots and fruit through the blender. Or she stands in the bathroom spraying some kind of tropical mess on her hair and squeezing the curls around her temples so they stay there without moving until she washes them out in the shower.

Cynthia's only true hobby outside of "creating an image," that's how she puts it, is collecting refrigerator magnets. Now, that isn't a true hobby, not like collecting baseball cards or refinishing furniture, but she has elevated it to that status, and who's to tell her it's silly. Not me. She's got so many of them doodads they cover both doors of the refrigerator, and just recently she's taken to putting them on the front panel of the dishwasher where they tremble through the scrub cycle. Our only true fight to this day was the one time I slammed the door to the icebox and half her magnets fell to the floor, two of them things cracking into pieces down on the linoleum, and she threw a fit like I'd never seen. Just like I'd stepped on her tail, hissing all ugly between her teeth with green facial clay wrinkling in cracks across her cheeks. Now that was a sight.

I've been promoted to crew chief for Clem Palmer's Asphalt and Paving out of Tyler, and we're tarring a stretch over to

Statesboro, so since she threw that hissy fit, I pick up a magnet for her here and there to add to her collection, just to show I care. Mostly I find ones of beer cans and Harley emblems, but I did find a real funny one at Red's store, a shiny naked ceramic lady with big pointed tits, holding her hands on her hips, and with a smile on her lips. Little black letters float across her shiny pink belly, saying, "Get a PIECE of the action," and now, I think that's real cute. Of course, Cynthia says it looks just like her, and a few days after I carried it home to her, she took to referring to me as her "fiancé." So, tell me how that works.

Now, Cynthia and Yolanda aren't nothing alike. Reason I got hooked up with Yolanda at all was out of sheer boredom with my regular type. That's no reason for starting up something like I did, but accidents happen, what can I say? That summer, I'd just broken off with Susie Purviss, who is now married to E. Henry Broadwell, who just happens to be working for Clem Palmer in payroll, but we don't have no bad blood between us these days. Susie had broken things off once E. Henry came around, seeing as she complained she was getting too old to just keep dating like we were, and how I should ask to marry her. She's a charge nurse there over to Reidsville now, pulling in a nice tidy check every week, but marriage was not in my mind two years ago, and it still isn't much in my mind today. Except for those times when Cynthia goes all throaty and says, "And I'd like you to meet my fiancé." Meaning me.

So, Susie and I'd broken up to her crying of "Why can't we just get married, Donnie?" and I certainly wasn't looking for something like that again, though to be honest, that is my pattern. I'm thirty-four, and for the past ten years it's been a woman a year, give or take a couple of dry months now and then. See, you start out saying, "Now, mind you, I'm not looking to settle down just yet." And you say it right from the jump, looking those straight-teethed girls dead in the eyes, and they go, "Why, whatever gave you reason to think I'd expect that from you, Donnie? Why, aren't you just the most nervous man I've ever met?" Then somewhere down the line, it changes. They start talking about moving in together, and they go all pink faced and smiling at babies in strollers, even the ones with spit and cereal leaking in a mess down their chins. They take to staring at you for long, silent moments across the table at the diner next to Miss Lucille's motel, like they was trying to read your mind. I'd just come out of a version of that and kicked around single for a couple of months, when right after the Fourth of July, I noticed Yolanda back of the bar, though she never so much as touched my fingers when I paid for my beer, not even handing back change. Like I been saying, she wasn't my regular type.

Most of the women I end up with are the kind that make certain you notice them first. They sit around on bar stools just crossing and uncrossing their legs, smiling those glassy smiles, shaking their hair off their shoulders. They sit there like there weren't the whole place studying their neat little bottoms, lifting their drinks to their pink lips just so slow it makes you wonder. They're the type once you finally get a couple of beers working, they start making conversation from down the bar or the next table, depending on where you're sitting. They're the kind once you're a little drunk it don't take nothing to talk to them, and they lean into you a little once you ask their names, like exchanging names was some kind of personal secret. They're the type once you've got their names straight like to go upstairs and shoot a little pool, only they don't really know how to shoot at all, asking, "Should I hit it here? There? Off the side, there? I couldn't do that, it'll never work," squealing, "Donnie, look it," all delighted when they sink something somewhere by accident. They're the type what been noticing you all along, but got it planned so when you finally park yourself next to them at the bar, when you finally look in their eyes, it's like you've just arrived on this earth, beamed down extra special just for them.

But not Yolanda. She'd come from school in Atlanta, where she'd been studying design, though what that meant, I wasn't quite sure. She'd come to live with her sister Regina, an interior decorating consultant, though later I'd find out they were both from that stretch on the Walapaha back home nobody ever mentions as a birthplace proper. The river spreads out back there so wide it seems like a lake when you stand there near the landing. I know the place good, even took a ride out there last spring with Teddy, Cynthia's brother-in-law, thinking maybe I'd catch sight of Yolanda. He's got that speedboat, blue metallic, and we drove on down to the landing one afternoon, down past Yolanda's mama's place, back through those trails don't even seem like a road to anywhere, but then the pines clear away and suddenly, there it is, the old shacks, even a couple of trailer-houses, though how they got those back in there is a mystery. Teddy and I took the boat on down where the Walapaha feeds into the Altmaha, then to where that river gets dark and the banks rise up, winding all through the woods. My daddy used to take me to the landing to get his liquor. They got a couple stills back in there, though to look, you'd never find them. The Feds come around every month or so, but the people back there are on to that, going so dumb and simple-acting you wouldn't think they'd ever done nothing but sit home all day and read the Bible, waiting for their welfare checks.

But that's something I found out later about Yolanda. The summer we met, I was working for Clem out of Savannah on a contract job at Hunter army airfield. I was putting in twenty hours overtime a week laying tar on a couple of runways, and the Tenderloin got to be my summertime watering hole. Yolanda was working there nights and living in an efficiency apartment over her sister's office in a three-story house two blocks from the bar. She'd had to find a place to work within walking distance of her apartment, since she'd slammed her car into a viaduct on purpose driving home from Atlanta. She'd just left it at the side of the road outside Macon, can you beat that? Unscrewed the plates and took the papers from the dash, then settled with the claims adjuster for cash money and left the car on the shoulder. "Better than being flat broke," she explained. And she took the job at the Tenderloin because it let her work nights and sleep through the day, and that was something she'd needed.

But like I was saying, I found this out later, because at first I just kind of kept noticing her, and she wasn't putting on no show for me. So I took to trying to get her to notice me, but she had this attitude about her like you didn't exist except as a body ordering beer. My regular tactics didn't have no effect, and if I'd try to wink her down for a draft, she'd come over to my table, saying, "What can I get you?" formal, without a smile, like I hadn't been a regular there for two months, part of the herd, and always drinking from the tap.

She wasn't my type, and I knew it. She was the kind you have to sideswipe into noticing you back, the kind you get a fix on, then let up on the gas and coast into. The boys in the crew seen it coming clear as day, saying how I ought not to mess with someone so serious-faced and unsmiling, and how didn't she look something like a witch. Trust us, they warned. But she got to me, in some deep place I didn't quite know about yet. If business was slow, she'd set up a stool behind the bar and pull out a sketchpad and go to drawing. And that's part of why business picked up for Willie B., in addition to Toujaise's band, because she drew anybody who walked in the door in two minutes flat, and she drew them perfect. She'd take out a piece of charcoal, a long, black stick-looking thing didn't seem no picture could come out of, and then she'd swing it across the page, scribble back and forth with it, work her fingertips in little circles to make shadows and what have you, and that was all it took. Magic. Darryl in his Atlanta Braves jersey, Toujaise in his beret at the microphone, Sasha holding her fingers across her mouth in that embarrassment she has about her overbite when she's not singing, the Wonder Bread man bringing in trays of kaiser rolls for the grill. She'd get the face down, sketch the shoulders real quick, collar, hair, and she'd put her initials at the lower right-hand corner and pin it to the wall near the register with a thumbtack.

About the third week she'd been working at the Tenderloin, I come in early on Friday. It'd rained all day, and I'd let the crew go at three. I come in the door and Yolanda was sitting back of the bar, and I said, "All right, go on now, go ahead."

And she says, "Go ahead, what?" standing up like she's going to get me a beer or something, moving slow and cautious, like I wasn't the sort to be trusted.

"Go ahead and draw me," I smiled, feeling a little silly, because she'd never taken to drawing me on her own, though I come in every night.

The place was real quiet and the jukebox was turned low with Roy Orbison crying about crying out the cloth speaker, and only some gay boys in leather jackets standing around at the back drinking beer and shooting darts. She looked at me then, holding her face in a frown, her hands stuffed down into the pockets of those baggy black pants she always wore. Her face was all white with some kind of powder, unnatural-looking in general, but nice to look at on her, just the same. She wasn't my regular type, but she was something to look at all right, even if she weren't the sort I had the habit of looking at in general, the kind I could take to measuring up in one or two glances, and learning everything I needed to get things rocking and rolling between us real quick.

Even how Yolanda done her face up with makeup was pretty, even if it was a little peculiar. She wore color on her lips what never rubbed off, and not appearing like regular lipstick, seeing's how it was dusty-like and dark as old blood, and real different from them shiny fruit-tasting colors what most girls went to sliding all over their mouths. All around her eyes was a thin black line I'd never noticed before, running narrow along them lashes what was all her own, and so naturally thick I wanted to reach across the oak planks of the counter and touch them.

Then she said, "Yeah. That's good," like she'd never really seen me before, pinching her eyes all tight and serious, studying me between them long fringes of her lashes, not like the type what pretends to just that moment see you, but in genuine blindness to the fact I'd even existed prior to that very second. With her staring me over like that, I got this helpless kind of feeling, like I'd just been born. Then she lifted up her face, looking me so hard in the eyes that I had to turn away for a moment. So, I stood there dripping rain onto Willie B.'s red carpet like some big fool in my steel-toed work boots, and she stood there examining me like that, not moving for a good long minute. Then she finally pulled out her sketchpad from next to the register, saying, "You got a name then?" and pointing for me to sit across from her there at the bar as I answered.

She sat behind the bar on that tall wooden stool Willie B. had bought special for her drawing, and I looked her over, really looked, not in the looking-to-pick-somebody-up kind of way, but seeing the narrow curve of her neck, the ridge of her spine, the way her head shadowed the sketchpad, seeing her scalp white like candle wax beneath her glossy black hair. She wore her hair poked up in a rubber band at the top of her head, like a little make-believe Indian feather, funny to do with hair short as a boy's, but it looked kind of nice on her. Little wisps of hair fell down on her white forehead and at the back of her neck. Then she said, "Don't look at me while I draw," even though she'd never looked up the whole time to see me looking. So I stopped looking at her, because I had been looking, she was right.

So I stared into the mirror behind the bottles of liquor back of the bar, and I could see her reflection next to mine, and I looked at that, the flat, pale face from the side, that little bit of nothing nose, hoops in her ears big around as beer cans, three in one lobe, two in the other. She was wearing a white T-shirt, the only thing I'd ever seen on her thin body, and she wasn't wearing nothing underneath, her small breasts barely showing except for the shadows of her nipples. She had a red leather belt through the loops at her waist, and a thong of keys hung to one side.

She held the charcoal in the tips of her fingers and used her left hand to make shadows by rubbing the edge of her palm against the page. Her hands were pale, and the nails were short and plain, trimmed, not chewed away like some girls do, what with always putting their fingers in their mouths. Her face was what got to me that day, so white she seemed not to be living, and that dark stuff on her lips making me want to kiss her, and maybe she felt that, who knows.

She sat there drawing a few minutes, and I'd thought she was done when she lifted up once to meet my eyes. "Hold still," she'd said, just ordering me around, though I didn't know I was moving. She bent back over the paper, and went to making just the tiniest strokes with the charcoal. Then she looped her initials into place at the bottom of the page and said, "There." She turned the sketchpad toward me then from her lap, and there I was, me, real as real. She'd got the scar at my lip just right, a shadowlike divot where I'd gone through the plateglass window at Mama's twenty years ago. She'd drawn me smiling, though I hadn't smiled the whole time she'd been working at the thing.

"Well," I said, grinning dumb-like. "Well," I grinned again, "Looks like me, don't it now?" I couldn't stop grinning, though I felt a fool for doing so, with my mouth stretched like a Band-Aid across my face.

Then she said real nervous-like and peculiar, "You like it, then? Tell me the truth." Her saying that was peculiar, as I'd never heard her ask that of anyone before, only heard her say, "See Willie B." when a customer asked to buy a likeness, only heard her say, "That's a five spot," when her drawing went public and all. But there she was, all quiet and anxious about her drawing for the first time that I'd seen, and boy, that did something to my heart, I can't tell you.

"It's great," I said, the grin of an idiot still expanding across my face. "I like it fine," I said, feeling myself go all tender and loose inside about her concern.

She tugged at the paper and ripped it from the pad. "Take it," she said as if she was mad at me and wanted just to be rid of it or something.

"I owe you some money, now," I answered, fishing my wallet by its chain from the back pocket of my jeans.

"No charge," she said, and then a smile shot to her lips, her teeth flashing all sudden in her small white face, like she just then figured out something important. "You remind me of someone," she smiled. "Take it. It's yours," she said, then a couple of men in three-piece business suits come in the front door, and she walked down the bar to serve them.

To this day that whole night sticks in my head like some movie I could've watched just this morning: Yolanda worked the bar until eight, then drew pictures for the customers brave enough to come in during the storm that worked itself into a fit after the sun went down. Around eleven, the electricity went out, and Willie B. set candles on all the tables, and the band come up and sat near the bar and two of them brought out acoustical guitars and made music real quiet up there at the front with Sasha singing. Willie B. didn't get no power the rest of the night and he let Yolanda off at midnight and she come and sat next to me at my table, where two guys from the crew sat drunk and not minding their manners much. She sat there next to me, not asking if she could, knowing as well as I knew that I wanted her there, small as a child, and quiet, her thigh light as a wing up against mine. She drank beer from the bottle with her lips pulling at the neck, and every once in a while would say something a little odd, like once asking, "You believe in voodoo?" which set us three drunk men into snorts. "No, really," she'd said. "You shouldn't laugh about something as serious as that," then she smiled real gentle, wrinkling her nose up in her face. Something she said set me back a little, though I was kind of laughing along with the other two guys from the crew. "My mama's a practicing witch," she said, and right after she'd said it a flash of lightning lit all the dark windows of the bar. Tony, one of the guys, went, "Oh my God," and Yolanda said, "See?"

I had a good-old-boy tired drunk going around one, and at closing asked couldn't I see her home, and she nodded without a smile to her white face. So we drove my truck the two blocks to her sister's place and she took me upstairs by the hand to her room where she slept on the floor on a mattress, the moon just barely cutting through the clouds after the rain, just coming in faint through the windows.

If you'd asked me that morning where I'd end up that night, I couldn't have guessed it'd be there under the cool sheets of her bed. I'd never have guessed I'd be lying beneath her as the wind come through the open windows, her thin legs at my hips, her lips opening against mine from the first kiss. I'd never have guessed things to go like that, not with her, not lying there letting her love me with her weightless body in the rain-washed night. She'd made love to me in absolute silence, kissing from my lips to my neck to my belly, then later, riding up above me, so light I could've lifted her in my arms. Only once did she say anything at all, and then it was only, "Oh, now," announcing the squeeze of her body.

When morning come, the room was closed up and dark. She'd gotten up before dawn to draw the blinds at the windows, and she slept beside me on her back with her hands at her chest. Her breasts were small and white, and the nipples lay flat against her skin. I kissed her breasts as she slept. I kissed her nipples to points and she reached her sleepy arms around me and I moved inside her a long time before I came, and she fell back off to sleep right after.

She kept her room dark in the day and at night opened all the windows. In a bowl beside the bed, she kept three pale stones, and each morning she warmed them in her palms and chanted over them in a trance, words sounding senseless to me, but pretty how they come out of her mouth. Once I visited her with a case of heatstroke, and she boiled herbs on the hot plate and made me drink the whole mess from a spoon. In an hour I was well, and I'd sat naked in a chair while she trimmed my hair, collecting the pieces she cut in an envelope, sealing it closed with a press to her lips.

We went on real regular that summer, her working the Tenderloin, me coming to see her at the bar after Clem called out quitting time, going home with her at closing. She never liked going out much during the day on the weekend, but I coaxed her into taking rides down the coast or up toward South Carolina, and sometimes the hour inland to Tyler. She didn't like Tyler. She said it was an old sore for her. So I asked her why. And that's when she told me she'd been born on the river, though all along I'd pictured her coming from the city.

Driving into Tyler one day she said, "Okay, we always go to your mama's house. Let's go to mine this time. See what you think." We drove back into the woods and down to the landing, the sky all blue and thin with clouds. There were girls swimming at the landing in their clothes, shorts and cutoffs, wearing little stretchy tops. A couple were pregnant, their white bellies popped out and showing. Yolanda called out to a few by name, and they come up to her and pressed her hand between theirs. One girl named Jasmine said, "Heard you're doing readings again." Yolanda nodded, then Jasmine said, "Well, what you said come true. My period come just regular. I was only late." Another girl stood at the edge of the river with a small, dark-haired child in sagging diapers pulling on her wrist. Yolanda called out to them.

"Hey," she said. "Hey, over here," she said, and the child turned from the girl at the edge of the river and walked up the beach to us. "Come on," she laughed to the child, and the child come running toward her, going, "Mama, Mama," laughter bounding all around in his chest from running on those fat, white legs, and Yolanda swept him up in her arms.

She held the child against her, nosing her face at his neck and kissing his shoulders, and my skin went a little cold. She looked up at me once, dead in the eyes and staring me down. Then she turned away from me and walked down a soft sliver of a path to a clapboard shed back of the tackle and bait store. I stood there on the beach and then followed behind her a minute later. She stood at the door to the shack and waited for me to catch up. "This is Joey," she said. "He's mine."

"You never told me," I said, brushing gnats from around my mouth. The insects buzzed in a cloud at our heads under the thick oaks above us.

"You never asked," she said without any kind of tone to her voice. Just, "You never asked," like maybe I was supposed to guess at her life and figure it out. "So, you going to stop liking me?" she said. She didn't say "loving me," and that made me feel all messed up inside.

"Well, I'd a rather known," I said, a little bit of anger seeping into my voice, anger come out of not knowing about this baby of hers.

"I see," she said softly, just like that. "You don't own me," she added, and then opened the screen door to the shack. I followed her inside, the door barely closing behind us as it was hung so rickety and poorly in its rotted frame. Inside the shack the walls were covered with feedbags, stapled to the wood in regular rows, like some kind of makeshift decorating. The shack was divided into rooms by mismatched paneling fixed to the floors and ceilings with metal angle brackets. A gas stove and sink stood at the front of the main room, and two curtains made doors to rooms in the back, though the whole thing was no bigger than a two-car garage. A thin woman sat at a gray formica-topped table in the center of the front room. Her hair was pulled back in a braid, and she wore a pink housecoat fastened with safety pins in the front. Her legs were white and thin, and small patches of broken veins flattened out under the skin. A hand-rolled cigarette hung from the left corner of her mouth, lips so pale I could barely make them out. She looked up when Yolanda and I come in the door, though she didn't give us so much as a nod. Then she looked down at the table in front of her where a magazine lay spread out to a picture of lemon chiffon pie. She looked back up at Yolanda, fingering the cross that sank between her breasts. Then she said, "Got the money, thank you," smoke from her cigarette coming out of her lips with the words. "Bought him diapers," she said, tearing the page from the center of the magazine, her long fingers working the paper free from the spine, the cross at her neck knocking against the table edge. "Don't let Nigel see you toting that boy in from town now, you hear?" I could tell the way she looked up at me quick when she said it who she meant.

Yolanda put the baby down at her feet, and he toddled over to the woman at the table and crawled up into her lap, leaning against her sagging bosom. Yolanda crossed her arms at her waist and stared at me for a moment, then back to the woman at the table. "Mama, Nigel don't want me," she said, her voice going dark in a way I hadn't heard before. "Nigel don't want us," she said.

"Nigel don't talk like that to me," said her mother, running her finger line by line along the recipe for lemon pie. "He know you left school to work in Savannah. He know you work at some place where queers go. He know you live up above your sister. He got spells going to bring you home. Ask," she stated, looking me over like I wasn't a living being. "Ask anybody here, they tell you the same."

"Nigel's got a new baby girl down the Altmaha," Yolanda said. "I don't want nothing from him, neither," she said, her voice sounding so much like her mama's I had to look to see if it was her talking at all. "Nigel ain't nobody," she said, turning to look at me real serious-like. "He's a bad kind of person. He runs people around here," she sighed. "I'm done with him. I got me a new life," she said softly, and it scared me to think she meant me.

Driving back to Savannah that night, Yolanda sat close to the door with her knees hugged up to her chin. Ten miles out of Tyler she said, "So, maybe I should have told you. So maybe I did, you'd leave me. Drop me. Stop liking me." She still wasn't talking about loving her. All she could talk of was liking.

So I go, "It's a lot to think about, I'll give you that. It's a surprise to me, what you having a baby and all. You don't look like you've had a baby. Your skin don't look stretched or nothing," I laughed, trying to cheer her up.

"I could've died with him," she said. "I was tiny and I could've died, except for Elvira's doctoring."

"You don't mean Black Bob's Elvira?" I exclaimed. "That nigger lady, that Elvira, that fat old nigger?"

She sat there in the quiet truck, looking straight ahead down the highway, but staring so hard didn't seem like she seen nothing but what was up inside her head. She stared straight into the night as we passed the forestry tower going eighty, where two army jeeps sat parked bumper-to-bumper at the mouth of the trail leading back into the woods. Alongside the jeeps, two soldiers in field helmets were pulling fire watch. The edge of my high beams washed across the ground at their feet and up the pines rising behind them, the embers of their cigarettes streaming by like two red eyes in the dark. She sat there with her knees up, then she turned to me.

"You white boys got the world all figured out, don't you now?" she said, her voice tight with anger. "You get born into decent families with money to get by on, with daddies who come home at night, daddies you known all your lives by name, thinking you belong to them daddies like something God shit out of gold. You think the only decent folks are white people like yourselves, and you call people like Miss Elvira "niggers," like they was something dead at the side of the road, like something without a heart or a mind. You play football and hang little cheerleaders on your wrist, and sometimes they let you feel their tits, but that's it. They don't let you do what you really want to do. So, white boys like you come prowling down by the river on Friday nights, and you find girls with dark eyes, and you buy their daddy's shine, and you get them to drink beside you in the woods, and you don't even remember their names the next day. White boys like you make babies and go away to school to nice places where you find some precious little someone to marry who's still got her cherry. Don't you call my family "niggers." Miss Elvira's blood. She raised my granddaddy at her breast when his mama died of fever, kept him as her own when wouldn't nobody claim him, a little white-baby, and she saw him get in bed with her own half-white daughter, but don't nobody know that side of it. You saw my mama. She's white-looking, now, isn't she? But that don't make me true white. Black men give babies to white girls down to the river. That don't mean nothing. Everyone acts so appalled into Tyler, like us river girls aren't nothing but animals, like we don't got hearts to break and bend. But, your daddies come poking around the river, looking for something they can't get at home, and they pay for black girls in Shanty Town, just the same as black men bring their money to us girls at the river. Don't talk to me about niggers, Donnie."

She stopped a minute then, leaving me stuck in silence behind the wheel, and my fingers took to shaking in pulling out a cigarette from the pack sitting inside my shirt pocket. She studied my face and my trembling fingers as I punched in the lighter on the dashboard, then she went on. "My mama's French, and her family come down here from Quebec way back. None of us got the same daddy, except for Regina and me. You want to know who our daddy is? You want to know what good Baptist come out to stick his thing in some poor white trash at the river? You want to know Miss Elvira's grandbaby's name?"

"Stop it," I whispered, seeing's I'd already heard more than I could even begin to puzzle out.

"No," she said, and so fiercely, I started shaking on the inside along with my fingers. "You need to know the truth, even the truth you can't half bear to hear or understand. You need to quit living your white boy life where the world's divided up into white folks and niggers. My daddy was old man Rogers, Louise's daddy, but you wouldn't have called him a nigger, seeing as only a quarter of his blood run true black, and he passed easy enough for white. He paid my mama to love him, then paid her to keep quiet once we come along. He come out to see her once a week all his life till he got the cancer. Louise maybe knows I'm her blood, the way she looked at me sometimes when she was selling cosmetics there into Danner's store. We don't got to say nothing, she just knows. Her daddy hurt her, you can see it in her face and how she don't need to name her own baby's daddy. But she was born there in Tyler, looking white and living white. Me, I look white. Mama's skin's so pale, guess it come down to me that way. My granddaddy got killed on the river, and I seen it, I seen the knife go clean into his heart. Some woman went wild on shine and poked him with a knife till the air whistled out his lungs and blood filled his mouth. Miss Elvira come out and buried him back in the woods, seeing's she raised him up at her breast like one of her own. Don't nobody ask questions about dead men down there."

I could feel how she was watching me then as I sat there, feeling how she'd turned just slightly to get a clear look at my face. She stayed quiet for a good long minute, and in the silence I got to feeling she was waiting for me to sort out and make sense of everything she'd said, but not seeming like she was sitting there expecting me to speak. Avoiding her face like I was, I kept feeling she knew how I didn't have nothing to say yet, even with me clearing my throat a couple times out of habit. "And let me tell you about girls like me," she said then, peering forward out the windshield again and her voice going low and sounding almost sad. "Sometimes we get free, go away, get jobs, get educated, but the river don't leave you. You seen Joey. I gotta live with that. I can't never be really free. And if you don't like me for that, I can't do nothing to stop it." Then she grew quiet, and I kept staring forward with the truck sailing on toward the coast.

My mouth had gone dry, and the cigarette burned hot at my lips as the ember reached the filter. I tossed it out the window, flinging it hard into the dry brush whistling by at the side of the highway, which was something dangerous and awful to do. "So, who is Nigel?" I said, my voice coming out my mouth high and fast. "Who's this Nigel? Some white boy?"

"He's not a white boy like you," she answered softly. "I don't love him no more," she added. That was the only time I'd heard her talk about love, and she never brought it up again.

"He's river folk. He lives most the time with a girl there to Jesup, but he's river people. And he put a spell on me early. I was only sixteen."

"A spell?" I said, and I laughed in disbelief. "A spell. Now, that's funny."

"You white boys don't know what that means," she whispered. "You don't have no way of knowing what that means. He put a spell on me," she said, looking over at me as I drove toward Savannah. "He got Old Jennie to take things from my mama's house, things that belonged to me, strands of my hair, dust from the corners, a patch of cloth from my bedsheets, and then he put a spell on me. You don't know what that's like," she said, her voice gone as thin as the air coming in the windows. "You don't know what it's like to find yourself possessed till you faint for wanting someone, faint for what comes into your head without knowing why. That's what a spell does, sends you out in the night till you find what you're looking for, till you fall down on your knees, the fire all hot inside your middle, like you were to die from it."

"So, where is he now?" I asked, feeling momentarily frightened, afraid maybe something might happen to me, to us, like maybe I'd find myself driving possessed, ramming into a tree or sailing off the side of a bridge. We were alone on that dark stretch of road. Anything could happen and be made to look like an accident, seeing's how I had this girl in the truck that Nigel had got under his spell enough to have a baby by him, whether I believed it or not.

"He's still around," she sighed, and then she yawned, real slow and stretching toward me across the seat like a pale night animal. Then she inched over beside me. "He can't get to me these days," she whispered, pressing her hand to my zipper.

"What about the spell?" I asked, trying to keep my voice light but feeling all heavy inside. I lifted my hips from the seat as she unfastened my jeans, keeping both hands tight on the wheel.

"It's been broken," she whispered at my ear right before she lowered her face to my lap. The moon hung like a gold plate over the low marshes and reedy banks that laced the river outside the city. The water on either side of the road lay still and black, mirroring the night on its surface. A crane lifted up from the side of the road, its wings pulling in slow strokes in the moonlight as Yolanda took me in her mouth. I trembled between her lips and put one hand to the back of her head, my fingers knitting down to her scalp, and I kept driving in toward the city, steering hard, oblivious and blind to anything but the heat of her mouth.

Later that night as we lay in her bed, the wind blew in so warm we didn't need no more than a sheet. I lay there and touched my hands to her face. She'd showered before coming to bed, and her skin was smooth and bare. She'd dusted her body with powder, and I ran my hands the length of her torso and then worked my fingers between her legs. "No," she'd said. "I don't want to do that."

"I want to return the favor," I smiled, thinking what she had done in the truck. But she pulled her hips back toward the wall and smoothed the sheet in a barrier between us.

"I just want to lie here beside you and think," she said. "I got too much to think about," she said, and then she closed her eyes. "Sometimes I get thinking so hard by heart skips a beat. Sometimes, even with my eyes closed, I can't stop thinking."

She fell off to sleep like that, with me staring at her face the whole time. She'd taken me so quick and hard in the truck that I couldn't have made real love to her if I'd wanted. I didn't have anything left. I wanted to touch her white skin, to look at every inch of her body in the light of the night, to find every inch I'd never been and kiss her in those places. But she slept beside me and I didn't touch her. I'd never felt like that before, wanting to make love to a girl without wanting it myself. It was a sad kind of feeling, and it kept me awake until three. Then I fell asleep beside her, my arm at her shoulder until she pushed it away in a dream.

After that night it was hard to leave her each morning. Every few weeks we went down to the landing and saw Joey, but we never took him with us anywhere, just sat with him there by the water. Some afternoons I sat with Joey under the pines by the tackle and bait store, buying him Coca-Colas and marshmallow pies while Yolanda went into her mother's shack and did palm readings. I had her read the flat of my hand one evening at the Tenderloin, right before last call as we sat side by side at the bar. She'd held my big hand in between hers, trailing her fingers against my palms and calluses. "You'll live a nice long life," she told me, the back of my hand against her thigh. "You'll go many places, but you won't always know where you're going or why." I asked her would I ever get married, and she said, "Not soon," and I laughed. Then she added, "And not to anybody you know yet," and I laughed again, though for some reason, it hurt me to hear that. One late Saturday afternoon we were there at the landing and some boys from Tyler come out and swam in the river. They knew me from around, but not one of them spoke to me, just gave me sideways glances and looked at Yolanda.

The first week in September I went into the Tenderloin on Friday afternoon, looking for Yolanda, like regular. Willie B. gave me a quick sideways stare when I come in the door, his face falling serious, and he got busy washing glasses as I dropped on to a stool near the register. When I asked where Yolanda was, he said, "Well, Donnie, she's gone back up to school." That was a hard thing to hear, and at first I thought he was mistaken. We'd been spending every night in her apartment, and that morning she'd nodded when I said I'd meet her at the bar after work. The way Willie B. told it, seems everyone knew she was leaving but me. Seems Nigel'd come in early a couple nights back, holding her against the wall of the pool room upstairs and saying something right up close to her face. No one could tell what he'd said, seeing's how he spoke so low and all. And nobody'd told me he'd been there, neither, but Willie B. said maybe folks thought I already knew, like maybe Yolanda had told me herself, but she hadn't. Even with all of Willie B.'s explaining, I kept thinking he'd got it wrong, and made him swear he was telling God's truth. "Donnie, I swear," he insisted, and just looking at his face let me know she was really gone.

I sat in my truck outside her dark apartment the whole night without sleeping, knowing all along I was waiting for nothing.

I was still sitting there the next morning when Regina came around, and I followed her up the steps and into her office, asking if maybe she could tell me what to do. Even as I went to asking if she could give me Yolanda's address or something, I knew things were bad, seeing's how she starting shaking her head right away.

"Just leave her be," she said in the cool of her blue-carpeted office beneath Yolanda's room, her voice floating at me in a river-born echo of her sister's. "She's got troubles enough, let alone some Tyler boy come hunting her down."

"I just want to talk to her," I said, standing there with my hands closed tight in my pockets.

Then Regina leaned back in her chair behind the desk and folded her arms at her waist. "What you have to say doesn't matter. Words can't bring her back." Then she looked past me, through the window behind me to the street. "What you going to say, Donnie, that you love her?" She lifted her head then, and her eyes hit me dead-center. "I'm going to give you some advice, and you'd do best to listen up. Leave her be," she warned me. "For good and completely, or Nigel will see that you do."

Come Sunday, I wasted up the day at the Tenderloin, hanging out with the half of the crew what weren't married. Willie B. himself walked over when I first come in, slinging the meat of one arm at my shoulders. "Anything you need, let me know," he'd said, but I couldn't think of nothing to say. I needed to keep drinking to keep from thinking, and I lost all then won back twice my paycheck shooting pool. Willie B. covered our tables, though I'd never seem him work that section before. Every half hour, he'd chug up the stairs, toting up trays of whatever we'd hollered down for over the railing of the balcony. He'd stick around a few minutes, emptying ashtrays and wiping down the mess at our tables, saying, "Boys, you wouldn't be gambling up here, now, would you?" and we laughed, since he'd already known the answer. Every third or fourth trip, he'd call out, "Hey, now, Donnie," checking up on me and avoiding my eyes.

We chased double shots with drafts all afternoon, and around seven I was bent over racking the balls on the green felt table when a cool-fingered hand touched to the back of my neck. I let half a minute pass, making busy with squaring the rack, then I pulled up straight and turned around. Nobody'd had to tell me who was standing there. Nobody'd had to tell me that tall, olive-eyed boy with black hair bound back in a leather strip and a rat-tlesnake skin around the brim of his hat was Nigel. I'd felt it in his fingers against the skin of my neck, and I seen it in his eyes, sure as shit. Even for all my drinking, I'd known who had come up behind me.

At first glance, he was nothing but a boy, wiry-looking, his two thin arms angling down bare and pale and smooth, his fin-gers strung loose in his belt. But you get to looking at a boy like that, and the clues start falling into place. You look careful enough, and it's there, the knife butt resting at the top of one boot, jeans tight as skin and faded in the half-moon pattern of what he's got waiting behind his zipper, the rise and fall of pulse showing through the dip of his throat. He was slim and long, standing so easy you might be fooled into thinking this was nothing but a friendly little visit. But if you knew how to look, you could tell every inch of him was wound tight with muscles, coiled tense and waiting. And I knew, even topping him by forty pounds, I'd never win if I fought him.

As we stood facing off, the boys went quiet and fell back around us, knowing as well as I did that a fight might erupt between the space of our bodies. We'd all been party to barroom punches in our days, and we knew all the signs. I stood there, knowing I was whipped without even a fair match to prove it. I stared into those eyes of his, and got this peculiar hot feeling under my skin that made me seem a fool for standing there. But I kept on staring into his almond-shaped eyes, the one on the left with a diamond-shaped patch of blood near the iris. I'd been staring for maybe two minutes when he tilted his narrow head, saying, "You got something to say to me?" 'Course I didn't, and I shook my head. I couldn't trust my voice to come out of my mouth.

"Well, I got something to say to you," he followed, low in his throat, spitting the words like a sick yellow dog. He pulled a cigarette from the pocket of his plaid shirt, the sleeves cut off ragged at the shoulders, showing the tight knot of biceps where Yolanda's name lay stretched out on the left across a heart red as new blood. They were professional tattoos, not the kind made in the middle of some drunk with a sewing needle and ink from the office supply store, real nice tattoos like the ones done in that parlor next to the front gates of the post, the one soldiers go to to have GOD-MOTHER-COUNTRY stenciled over their chests, going into the flesh the way those words are already deep in their actual beating hearts. He took a Marlboro in his fingers, twisted off the filter, and stuck it between his pink lips, the flesh of his mouth sweet as Joey's and teeth so white they didn't seem right in that poor-boy's face.

"Well, now," he said, holding a silver lighter to his face, flicking it once so the flame wasn't quite touching the tobacco. Then he sucked in hard so the fire pulled to the tip of the cigarette and caught. The crew was behind me. I couldn't see them, but I heard them breathing close at my neck, so it didn't feel so bad having to face this boy like that eye-to-eye. But even with the boys there behind me, I couldn't keep my hands from trembling in my pockets. "Well, now, I've been wondering what someone like you might look like," he smiled around the butt of the cigarette, talking smoke out of his lips. "You ain't soft like I thought you might be. Suppose that comes with working asphalt," he said. Then he lifted his head real quick, and all that pretend niceness dropped from his face, and all his energy went to his eyes in a squeeze.

"If I hear you're trying to find her, I'll see you don't walk for a year. I'll see you don't walk or talk or have nothing left between your legs what works," he said in a snake of smoke. "And I'll see she don't neither," he added, then he took the cigarette from between his fingertips and dropped it to the carpet. He stepped on the butt without lifting his eyes from my face, stepped on it exactly where it fell by my feet, never looking to see where it landed. "I'll take that baby and she'll never see him again," he continued. "Lots of nice white folks'll pay cash for a baby sweet as that one," he grinned, so wide I could see the pink of his gums. Then he turned, looking once over his wild-horse shoulders at me and the boys standing there dim-witted by the pool tables, not one of us breathing regular.

LOVE'S A funny thing. Cynthia and me been together just shy a year now, and I know what's coming up next. She'll keep calling me her fiancé. She'll keep introducing me like that to her friends and the people we meet when we go into Tyler. And then someday I'll just tell her that's not what I got in mind, and she'll go to crying and buying me cards with all kinds of sweet talk and flowers and hearts printed on the front. Then someday when I'm too hungover to be patient with her, maybe I'll slam the refrigerator door so her all-important magnets go flopping down on the floor, and she'll say something like, "See, I don't matter to you." And maybe she'll cry and maybe she'll throw something. Maybe she'll break a glass against the wall. That's how those things happen.

I haven't heard from Yolanda and don't know what I'd do if I did. I found out she's still at that school in Atlanta because she made the front page of the *Tyler Sentinel* with a show she put on at a gallery in Norcross. They ran her picture on the front page, and she looks the same as ever, standing in front of her pictures all hung on the white wall of some building, and the show was called "White Boys and River Girls." The paper didn't actually mention her drawings, but I wouldn't expect that they would, everything considered. Yolanda's not smiling into the camera, but I wouldn't expect that neither. She was a pale slip of white trash back in Tyler, somebody nobody'd ever remember from high school, not even finishing proper, just taking her general education degree out of night school like misfits and pregnant girls do. She was one of those girls that we wouldn't recognize proper on the street, the kind we'd search out in a drunk and forget about sober. Seeing her face on the front page of the weekly paper made me feel guilty and ignorant all over again, like I'd felt that night in the truck.

The article running alongside the photograph had a title saying, "Local Girl Wins Major Award," and that seemed a sorry thing. She isn't true local, and she isn't a girl, not proper, seeing the article states she's twenty-two this year. But Tyler reclaimed her in her moment of accomplishment, and if Yolanda took time out to pose for the camera and answer questions for the reporter, then she must've felt right for doing so.

I keep the article in the top dresser drawer in our two-bed-room apartment. Cynthia asked once why I kept it, and I told her I knew Yolanda from the Tenderloin. Seems she'd have some knowledge about things, since we both know all the same people. But Cynthia don't ask what she don't want to hear.

I think about getting married, someday, not to Cynthia, but to who, I don't know. Late at night, I've taken to leaving Cynthia at home where she don't even notice I'm gone for all the image creating she does, what with *Vogue* and *Glamour* and *Elle* all open in front of her on the coffee table with the television on, nail polish bottle going clickety-click as she shakes it next to her face in one hand, punching buttons on the remote control with the other. I drive out toward the coast, across the causeways toward Tybee Island, and the lights from the truck slide over the water beneath and beside me. And those nights I get to thinking how time passes so quick you don't even know it's gone, how things happen you can't explain.

I keep a rabbit's foot on my keychain these days, and it hangs to the side of the steering wheel. I reach up to touch it every now and again, just quick. If you'd asked that summer if I loved Yolanda, I would have shot back fast that I wasn't the marrying type, like love and marriage go together in answering that question. But it's funny, because when I think of her face rising up like the moon over mine, when I think of her sleeping next to me there in her dark apartment, those cool smooth stones in the bowl beside the bed, something like love comes to mind.

I get in my truck and drive places without knowing where I'm going. I put my foot to the floor and open her up, trying to outrun the inside of my head, trying to shake loose of that kind of thinking.

I sit there driving, downing a cold one, going through a six-pack, stopping to piss at the side of the road, like maybe a drunk will stop me from thinking, like maybe I could forget, but I can't. I can't shake thinking about her. I don't want to tear loose of thinking about her, like it's some kind of spell. And I get to thinking maybe she's got a strand of my hair stuck away in her jewelry box, thinking maybe at night she pulls it out and warms it between her fingers, speaking over it on her knees, pulling forward in the pale curve of her narrow back. I think of those words in the breath between her lips, a slip of my hair at her fingertips, praying in river girl tongue.

MY NAKED BEAUTY

I'm thirty-eight, and I no longer know how to mother my daughter Corinne. She's just this month turned sixteen. Had I known what sharing a house with a pubescent, hair-spritzing, mirror-mated beauty pageant contestant would mean in the long run, however, I'd have stopped her cold. For now, it helps to keep things in perspective. Two doors down from us, Rhoda Emmons's fifteen-year-old Tammy is pregnant and keeping the baby. Jenna Browning hit a tree going eighty while drunk. She would have graduated next year with Corinne. For now, I remind myself that the contest at least fills up the days of her summer vacation. It keeps her out of the video arcades and away from the backseat of some boy's loud car and fast fingers. And after the pageant, I'll have my daughter back. Knock on wood.

For the most part, I don't think she's actually enjoying the competition, and why should any of us do something we can't at least like or be proud of? At the very minimum, a little tickling thrill or a twitch of joy. Of course, try to talk to her about the objectification of women, and she gives me her recently perfected "Get a life" look and a two-note dismissal of "Mo-ther." She sniffs at sisterhood. "Germaine who?" she complains when I suggest books for her summer reading list. "This," she tells me, "is life at its best. This," she tells me, "is dog eat dog."

"Well, little poochie," I chide, "then why is your hair falling out?" I've been sworn to zip-locked secrecy about this sad fact of balding. For now, she's concealing the status of her scalp under baseball caps and bandanas, praying for a miracle of restoration by pageant night. "Pray hard," I tell her, as the pageant's just three weeks away. The hair loss started two weeks back, and the doctor has diagnosed her condition as bona fide alopecia symptomatica. The most logical explanation for her victim-of-radiation appearance is the stress of competition, but she won't hear a word of that. She is choosing to blame her doggie-show-contestant mange on a dietary insufficiency of calcium. Now, due to the half-dozen small, white, fishmeal Hindenburgs she swallows with meals of cucumber slices and melba toast, she also has gastric distress. If she isn't upstairs in the bathroom, alternating applications of aloe vera gel, cortisone cream, or vitamin E to her scalp, she's on the couch with the heating pad clutched to her stomach. She sits there chewing Amphogel tablets while watching videotapes of pageants she ordered on my American Express account.

The worst thing about it is that one moment, there I was French-braiding her hair every morning, enmeshed in the secret sorority of shared menstrual cramps, with no dark cloud foreshadowing doom. One moment, I was just learning to delight in the ghost of my adolescent face emerging from her genetic map of bones and flesh, and the next thing there's a hair-shedding zombie at her place in the breakfast nook. "Excuse me, but do I know you?" I inquire, coming down for breakfast as this creature bites into a rice cake. She stares out from the narcotic of a Merle Norman mint-julep face mask and aims a pistol squirt of Giorgio behind each ear. While well-scented, she is at times deaf, dumb, and blind.

We've quit trying to talk about the things we no longer agree on. We sigh a lot. She sighs in eye-rolling dramatic contempt at the black nest of hair under each of my arms. The sight of my thatched shins is enough to send her into spasms of "Gross, God, gross, no wonder Dad left you." I haven't bought a razor in ten years. My own sighs are a groan of maternally stifled anguish each time I glimpse the waxing moon of her head. To add to this grief, she is, at this moment, lodged in the temple of our upstairs bath, plying a tube of bikini-line hair remover, denuding the remaining and more resistant swatches of her bodily fur in grand and stoic preparation for the Miss Chidler County Beauty Pageant. And for this, I went through Lamaze, Montessori, and Girl Scouts.

I teach writing and women's literature at the community college across town. Corinne's set on going to flight attendant school in Los Angeles once the pageant is over. "College?" she shrugs from time to time. "Like, there's no law that says everybody has to go to college," she announces.

Women, I tell her, need to establish self-sufficiency. "Like you?" she mocks in macabre laughter filled with all kinds of, what I consider, unwarranted implications.

Last night she practiced her dance routine in the living room until two, in a black push-up brassiere and pink spandex clamdiggers. This is the getup she'll wear when she prances and shimmies on stage. When I commented, as discretely as is possible in discussing aspects of reproductive anatomy, on the exhibition beneath the elastic fabric at the fully articulated vortex of her legs, she said she can't wear panties. They'd show under the cling. "Like, I mean, like don't you know anything?" she scolded. Of course I don't, I sneered. All I know is how to teach, how to raise two kids, how to keep this show on the road, how to pay bills, how to feed us. "Jesus," she meowed. "You're like, *so* archaic." She's got black velvet come-get-me stilettos to finish it off, and I just don't know how to like what she's doing.

Her father lives in California, which she says is "Absolutely too cool, like if I lived out there I wouldn't like have to send for everything like special order. Like, you can go shopping and everything there. Like the girls out there all have cars." All Richard says about the pageant is, "Send pictures."

So now she comes down the stairs in full regalia, taking the steps on display. She moves to the fanfare in her head, spine erect, as if Bert Parks himself is waiting next to me by the microwave cart. She comes at me with her thigh-swinging, synchronized-from-the-hip socket, runway walk, into the imaginary rolling surf of applause, into the middle-class reality of our townhouse kitchen, and she's wearing a royal blue bathing suit.

This suit makes my stomach buckle. Her heels lift her rump in a high-arcing prime cut. The flesh of her hips rises up, like the back end of some teenage boy's jacked-up Camaro. "I don't know you anymore," I say, turning from the sink. I'm washing three days' worth of dishes, the dishes she should've washed the day before yesterday. I am soaking milk from the bottoms of glasses. All household duties have been put on hold for the rituals of pageant preparation.

"Mother," Corinne says in a force of vexation, and then she stands there and starts pouting a little. The pencil-sketched sheen of her fuchsia lips bunches in a surrealistic flower beneath her nose. Her face is powdered chin to brow into milky porelessness. "The suit is a one-piece," she explains. "Who's kidding who?" I counter. There is only a G-string thong below the waist and two narrow shining triangles holding her breasts in place, body parts she did not inherit from me. I am the queen of the double-A bosom who never reached B status, even while pregnant or nursing. I wonder at times if she's still a virgin.

"Do you notice anything different?" she asks then, her voice dropped one worried note short of playful. At first I look down to where she's tugging at the crotch of her dubious attire, thinking maybe that's a clue for this worldly version of "I spy with my little eye." The white sheen of her thighs spreads in hairless, vulnerable blue-veined wings on either side of the loincloth. I stand there watching as she snaps the suit into its narrow definition of decency then draw back a few inches as she extends her face toward mine. I have a line of sweat on my upper lip. My skirt has adhered to my hips and the back of my legs, and I smell like bad cottage cheese. It's ninety degrees in the kitchen, and my daughter is offering me her face. A three-second count and then I have it. She's wearing green contact lenses.

"Your eyes," I say, drying my hands on the towel she cross-stitched for me only last Christmas, when the two of us had something in common, its purple floss declaring "The best man for the job is a woman." I sit at the small, white, formica-topped table and put my feet on it. Her waist is smaller than the top of my thighs. She's had her eyelashes darkened and her eyebrows lightened. She's become an illusion.

"I'm going to win this thing," she says, then turns on her blue satin pumps and walks show-horse stately to the refrigerator. She's singing "Wild Thing" under her breath, the song she's performing her routine to for the talent competition, and she's moving her hips in a genuine bump and grind the whole time. I have to close my eyes. Eight years of financing ballet lessons, eight years of Danskins and lambswool and toe-shoes, and out of it comes a skin-headed, neo-Nazi Charo.

Life wasn't always like this. I married her father, Richard, the last year of graduate school in Michigan. He'd taken a master's in electrical engineering, and I'd studied literature. I ended up teaching, but someday I'll buy a stone cottage out east. I'll write every night till the sun comes up and my hair grows in white, about what it is I don't yet understand that we give away giving birth.

Back in college, even with our divergent fields of study, Richard and I were more alike than not—at that point, at least. We liked old cars, old movies, old houses, old clothes and became, through necessity, quite fond of making do. Those early years, first with Corinne in her stroller, and then with Todd taking her place, were filled with long passages of contentment, of late afternoon walks in the park, with a simple sense of "We are going where we are going in no big hurry." Both of us took jobs in Cincinnati. The city was hilly and comfortable and our jobs were exactly what we had wanted them to be, challenging and also secure. And I suppose what happened to us, if one can ever truly figure these things out, is that I did not change as Richard changed: he became a lover of things—cars, computers, thermal insulating windows, German coffee makers, video cams, small foreign cars, investments—and I didn't. He moved to southern California. I boxed up the house and trucked us to the top east fingernail of the lower peninsula to teach.

I suppose if I had to supply some sort of explanation for anyone, I could haul out the photograph albums that I have so sentimentally maintained for the children and point to the demise of our marriage. It's portrayed in historical exactness— Richard in his three-piece gray suit at the Midwest Engineers' Seminar in Chicago, me at the Illinois Writers' Guild Workshop in my batik wrinkly skirt and khaki tee the same year. Richard receiving the Young Innovator's award at the Toledo Conference for Computer Research, me in my flannel shirt under the pear tree by the chicken coop at the old farm we rented across the river from Cincinnati. The last picture of the two of us together was taken at a faculty picnic where Richard stood like a poker-assed rigid soldier beside me on the dock of the canoe livery while I pretended to push him into the river: he did not participate in that charade. The pictures establish what happened: I did not keep step with my husband. I did not engage him in his quest for self-betterment, as he put it. I believed I was good enough then, and still do.

Neither one of us has remarried, though he's been living for close to three years with Melody, a twenty-nine-year-old systems analyst, with what I'm certain is a surgically buoyant bosom, as well as whatever's been injected to form the pliant half moons of her petal-pink lips. They both drive Saabs, which Corinne now believes is the ultimate symbol of sophistication. I've been driving the same car for six years, and I've always held the theory that all Saab owners are latent farmers. After all, with their industrial strength and legendary life spans, Saabs are no more than tractors with quarter panels. Todd and Corinne live with me for eleven months out of the year and spend July in California in the white stucco house Richard bought in San Diego. That is where Corinne decided, under the terra-cotta tile roof of her father and his limber-lipped lover, to play slave to the beast of beauty. That is where, last month, under the careful tutelage of Melody, my daughter laid plans to enter the pageant, ostensibly to earn a scholarship for flight attendant school, but if any money is made, it should just cover the bills she's incurred in becoming a mystery to me.

TWO DAYS later I come home from work to Corinne in the back-yard on the chaise lounge, a bottle of motor oil open beside her. I have seen this before. From the upstairs window of her bed-room comes a radio heartbeat of bass line across the yard. It's just after two, and this is where her daily agenda lands her, from noon to three, if there's sun.

My daughter's glorious form is encased in a chartreuse bikini of yore, dangerously outgrown, and smudged at the edges and openings with a margin of Valvoline. She has closed her eyes to the melanomic threat of the white summer blaze, and Bess, her best, same-size, sweater-swapping friend of eight years, is belly down in a Speedo on a towel in the grass beside her. My arrival, a two-block walk from the city bus stop, has gone unnoticed. They are lost in the world of a passionately flowered paperback, from which Bess is making a dramatic delivery, projecting her voice toward Corinne's dormant form, which, due to the tender skin of her nearly bare head, is crowned by a knotted scarf.

Gracefully, she has rotated her limbs into the optimum angles for exposure. She lies, palms up on the armrests, knees bent and parted, her eyes pinched shut in the solar swath, while Bess attends to the reading out loud of steamy couplings.

The book bears a metallic violet title. *Savage Garden of Hearts* undulates across a lush and blossoming background. Beneath the promise of this purple calligraphy stands a black and mus-cled stallion with loose reins, and beside him a blond man with wind-troubled locks. This man is wearing the customary jodh-purs and open-necked Elizabethan tunic, and is turning to look behind him, past the alps of his shoulders, toward the feminine figure near the towering oaks in the upper right-hand corner. In the midst of the muted floral backdrop, this vision is dressed for distress: draping red gypsy skirt—complete with ragged and sullied hem—the edge grasped in her gentle hands, delicious stretch of white thighs, tiny feet and toes, the requisite exposed shoulders rising up from the bodice of a marginally secure peasant blouse. And yes, those standard, gravity-resistant breasts are present and accounted for. Maybe even a shadow of nipple—in this light I can't tell. A man, a horse, a damsel—I prefer not to imagine the combinations.

The thrill of the story has allowed me an invisible box seat. As I stand at their feet, Bess emotes from center text. "'It was nearly midnight and raining when he found her there in the chill of the old stone church. She was sleeping gently on the floor with her cape drawn up to her chin. He knelt beside her and kissed her white forehead, and she woke then to welcome him near. She did not pull away from him as he pressed his heat against her. She opened the flower of her love for him. When the proud trumpet of his manhood announced his joy, she showered his shoulders with tears.'" Bess stops then and looks up at my daughter with a pleating wrinkle of her little nose. She pulls at the elastic edge of her bathing-suit bottom where it's riding up her rump. "Well?" she says.

"'The flower of her love'?" Corinne says. "'The proud trumpet of his manhood'?"

"'The proud trumpet of his manhood.'" Bess confirms, referring momentarily to the page, and then looking up into Corinne's closed-eye concern.

"What the hell's that supposed to mean?" Corinne complains. "Like, Jesus, did they do it or not? Is there any more?"

Bess speed-reads down the page, flips to the next, and goes, "Okay, here. There's more."

"Well, go on, already," sun goddess Corinne orders.

Bess takes a breath and dives back into emoting. "'In the

morning the sun poured through the stained glass and fell across their faces. The sword of his desire rose in male heat, and she lay beneath him, coming awake with the world and the woods beyond.'"

"Is that it?" Corinne asks.

"Yes, that's it," Bess sasses. "End of chapter, kaput, a little in and out business, and voilà, two happy campers." She presses the book closed between her palms and winds up her mouth in a drawstring against the shine of rubberbands and braces.

"Now, that is dumb," Corinne says. "Like, that is the most dumb thing ever, like why don't they just say it? Like 'the sword of his desire,' like it's some snap-on attachment." She is quite unhappy about this "male sword" business.

A look of calculated whimsy plays across Bess's face, and she goes, "Yeah, like imagine, 'Honey, would you hand me my male sword?'" Corinne gives a snort through her nose. It's almost a laugh. Bess is a good sort. Her mother is four times divorced, and Bess knows the truth about all the stuff this book isn't telling. "Like, 'Oh me, oh my,'" she continues, "'now where did I put my proud trumpet of manhood? And just when I need it most.'" Corinne rips off a true gut howl at this. This is very funny stuff, this trumpet.

"Where do you find these things?" Corinne asks, smiling with her eyes glued shut to the sharp glint of day.

"My mom's bedroom," Bess sighs.

"Figures," Corinne says in that smart-assed tone I won't tolerate in the house.

"Well, what do you expect from the marathon marriage

queen? Chaucer? Honestly, she's just my mom. I don't buy these things, I just read them. So anyway, what's your mom read?"

Corinne holds absolutely still for a moment, then relaxes back in the lounger. "Boring stuff. You know, stuff about feminist theory. You know."

"Bor-ing," Bess says in a foghorn. "At least she talks to you," she adds, and I smile. "My mom's got this new boyfriend. Hank. He's got a carpet-cleaning business. Every morning he gets out of bed and turns on country western and sings."

"Gross," Corinne comforts.

"Hi." I say from right stage, emerging from my invisible station. "I'm home from the front."

"Mom," Corinne says, sitting up in a struggle. She runs her eyes from my sensible shoes to my hairy calves and then reaches for the motor oil in the grass. Bess smiles and tucks the book under the edge of her Budweiser towel.

"Where's Todd?" Usually he's out in the street on his skate board, courting premature death.

"In the kitchen with Dede and Emilio and Stanley. They're working on that science club thing," Corinne answers, dribbling a thread of oil from the Valvoline bottle into the cup of her palm.

"What science club thing?" I implore, placing my hand in a visor above my eyes as I look toward the back door. Four dark figures are seated at the table beyond the screen.

"That radio thing. You know, that solar panel radio thing." She transfers the pool of oil in her hand to her belly in one quick sweep and then rubs. "Mom," she says, looking up at me. She sets down the grease and picks up a spray bottle of water. "Mom," she repeats, pumping the trigger from her toes up her legs. "Mom," she says a third time, "Todd and Dede are getting serious." Now she is misting her arms, then she turns the bottle on her face. She opens her eyes in a flutter of water-beaded lashes and says, "Today when we came in they were going at it on the couch."

"Going at it?" I ask.

"Like they were completely dressed and everything. But still."

"Todd's a good boy," I say.

"Hey," she says in sudden daughterly protection, something I don't hear much of these days. "Don't look like that. It wasn't anything really awful. It's just, like, Mom, he's not just a boy anymore. Right, Bess?" she says, poking her friend in the side with her orange-nailed jellybean toes.

Bess lifts up just long enough to give me a smile, then goes back to studying her patch of grass. "Well, he's very cute," she says. "It's just like all these girls think he's a babe. It was just like sort of embarrassing, you know, walking in on them. Maybe you should get him some books about it," she suggests.

"Bess, books? Jesus," Corinne chides. "Like, how lame. We have books," she says. Without makeup, with her tender head tied up à la Carmen Miranda, she is truly delightful to look at.

"How long were they alone?" I ask in an unwelcome flux of worry.

"Don't get all bent," Corinne says. "I mean, like I just thought you should know. Anyway, last month in California Dad tried to talk to him," she smiles. "No, listen," she orders. "This is something good. Like we're on the beach and there's these bezillion half-naked bodies, and Dad, like he goes, 'Hey, Todd, maybe you can grab one of these surf bunnies and go for broke.' Like I'm listening and all, and Dad's going around with his tongue hanging out, and Melody's telling him to plug his eyes back into his sockets, and Todd, well, like, he just gives Dad this look. So Dad goes, 'Pick one. Any one. Give her something to smile about,' and, gross, yeah, like I know. So Todd looks at him for a minute then says, 'What do you know?' That was it. Just, 'What do you know?' It was so cool."

The top-forty radio emissions break into a frenzied pitch for Cedar Point from the window. The deejay's voice is racing frantically across the yard. "See?" I grin. "He's a good boy."

"Mother," Corinne bellows over the carnival-noise radio as I turn and start walking toward the door. "Todd's not just a boy anymore."

I stop for a moment on the sidewalk, then turn back to the sunbathing beauties. Bess is sitting up now, unrolling aluminum foil and placing it under her legs. "I'll talk to him," I say as Bess slides a noisy rattle of silver under her left thigh.

"About what, exactly?" Corinne asks sternly. "Don't tell him I told you." She pushes the top of her finger under her turban and scratches.

"Oh, I don't know," I smile. "Maybe I'll talk to him about proud trumpets of manhood. Maybe about swords of desire."

Corinne turns to Bess in a flinch. "Ohmigod!" she cries.

"Ohmigod!" Bess echoes as they bend into squealing disbelief.

BESPECTACLED DEDE greets me from the kitchen table. "Queen Bee," she smiles from the chair, her legs wrapped around the rungs, the cushion of her rump wedged to the ladder-back. The "Bee" is for Beatrice. The "Queen" is for fun. Dede herself is a lively sort. She's Amerasian, born in Seoul to her Marine Corps father and his Korean wife, and she's lived all over the world and gets Todd to eat kimchee.

Todd's hit six feet this summer, and his metabolism has gone into hyperdrive. He eats three squares a day and fuels himself from meal to meal with chips, Oreos, white bread and bologna sandwiches, none of which appears on his narrow, neat body. Dede and I both bemoan the unfairness of his adolescent ability to graze without penalty. At four foot ten, she worries about her weight. She's thick in the waist and full breasted, but compact and dense with muscle, and she's always in motion. She met Todd three years ago and taught him how to skateboard. Last spring they both made the swim team. She also tutored him through calculus and got him to join the debate club. Just last week MIT informed her that she qualified for early admission, and her plan, all along, has been that Todd should follow her there.

"Mom," Todd says, looking up through his veil of blonde bangs. His fingers are pressed to a circuit board on the table, and Emilio is soldering a point on the map of wires and silver beads between Todd's fingers.

"Ma Bee," Emilio says in a chipped-tooth grin. He lost half a tooth last spring, wiping out on his skateboard in front of the mall. He didn't cry until I got him in the car. "Ma Bee, we almost got this thing so it works," he says. Since the accident I've been Ma Bee. He's holding the soldering gun to a silver pellet on the board. "You get an earful from Corinne?" he teases, elbowing Todd in the ribs. "She tell you she walked in on this Romeo?"

"Shut up," Todd says, head down over the table. He picks up a sandwich half from beside the board, and takes two bites from the center.

"Bee, you don't have to worry," Dede says. "About us, that is." She looks up at me and adjusts her glasses at the bridge of her nose. While her father is a heavy-faced man of Italian descent, she's inherited her mother's milk-glass skin. Her features, the quick rise of her nose, the subtle pleat of her dark eyes, suggest only a filtering of her Asiatic heritage. She is her mother's daughter from the neck up. Her body, she complains, is her father's. "Todd and I got big plans," she says. "Corinne, well." She pauses, thinking, then says, "Well, Todd and I have limits. Corinne doesn't know that, but we do. Right, Todd?" she says, and Todd begins nodding his head.

Todd looks up at me then through a swing of his hair, still nodding as he squints one eye. Stanley is five feet behind him, standing at the doorway in a Detroit Tigers cap, one of the three or four hundred Todd says he's collected and nailed to his bedroom wall. The cap with its orange D faces backward, and his headphones are hanging from his ears upside down. He's got his hands to the screen, fingering the mesh like a keyboard and humming as he makes an assessment of the girls on the lawn.

When Todd first started bringing Stanley around two years back, he'd struck me as some version of dangerous, which for those with daughters implies dangerously handsome. Later on I'd been relieved to find out that his father is a plastic surgeon and his mother plays viola with an East Coast symphony. While I have yet to meet his mother, as she's gone forty weeks a year on symphony tours, his father's come into the house several times. He's the kind of man who likes to meet his son's friends and their parents, and not at all what I'd expected of a surgeon whose specialties are tummy-tucks and face-lifts and elevated bottoms. He's quiet like his son, but with a gentle-voiced easiness Stanley lacks. And he sags. I'm embarrassed to confess I make a habit of noticing the draping of his flesh, and my guess is he's at some point past sixty. We should all feel free to flap and droop and turn to Jello as we please at that point, surgeon or not.

Part of the reason Stanley appears so deceptively disengaged with the world has to do with being smart, but I'm almost sure it's also part of growing up without his mother around. Even the months she's not touring with the symphony, she's busy with private students or flying off to give lectures, which explains why he likes the noise of our home. He spent his childhood in boarding schools, first in Switzerland, then in England, and I've learned he doesn't like to talk about what that was like. "It's not all that great," he's said the only time I asked him to tell me about studying abroad. "It's quiet," he added, and after that I never mentioned it again. Even without his mother to keep house and play mommy, he's inherited her talent, and he cringes when people compare him to her. He plays the piano and cello, though he's shy about performing and dropped out of the school orchestra. According to Todd, he'll be graduating a full year early, which isn't surprising, as he speaks four modern languages and Latin, and can hack his way into Harvard and Yale databases even I can't get to. He's got an auburn ponytail running straight down the middle of his back, a silver cross in one ear, and a black widow tattooed across his right wrist and knuckles. Todd laughs when I comment on Stanley's appearance and tells me it's an act. He says when a kid's so smart, sometimes he has to play dumb or the world's always asking for something. He says after a while, Stanley gets tired of being in the center, and all he really wants is to be able to hang out like everyone else.

Right now he's hanging out in the doorway with a hand on either side of the frame, and he's doing upright push-ups. "Man, they got some serious pan frying going on out there," he shouts over the music going into his ears. "That is some major kind of charbroil, all right."

"Mom," Todd says, looking from Stanley to my face and smiling. "Corinne's okay. She just feels like she has to report to you. Dede and me, well, we're for real. Don't worry."

"I won't," I say, easing my shoes off and shaking my hair from my neck.

"See?" Dede says. "See, Todd? No biggie."

"No biggie," I agree. "Now those two in the yard . . ." I sigh.

"It's a free world, man," Emilio says, holding the soldering gun to his temple. "This is America, dudes."

"No, man," Stanley laughs, pointing to Emilio. "Don't do it man."

"You'll all be sorry," Emilio cries out to us.

"Call 911," Dede grins.

"Don't kill yourself in my kitchen," I call behind me as I walk upstairs for my afternoon bath. "I'm too tired for a suicide today. Maybe tomorrow."

"Hey, man." Emilio shouts after me. "But you're letting those two babes burn to death out in the yard. We're talking self-immolation. We're talking Joan of Arc. What's the difference I solder my brains out inside?"

"You tell me," I yell back.

EARLY SATURDAY morning I wake from a dream to the shadow of Corinne at the foot of my bed. Customarily, I sleep until ten on the weekends. But the dreaming my daughter interrupts, that of my teeth falling out at a faculty meeting in great hunks of porcelain and amalgam, is gladly surrendered at just after seven. Wrapped in a navy blue robe, a towel around her neck, Corinne needs only a scythe to complete her grim-reaper appearance.

"Mom," she says. "What am I going to do?" The room is dark, only a bit of light coming in around the closed blinds, but I can tell from her voice she's been crying.

"About what?" I inquire, shaking the dream off and rolling to switch on the bedside lamp. In the thirty seconds it takes my eyes to adjust to the light, my question is answered. Her hair has dwindled to a few random baby-fine wisps. Beneath this halo of maize, her face floats opalescent, larger than life. "I see." What I see is the reality of her head. What I don't see is why she has to go through this.

"The other girls are going to find out," she says, then begins crying with her hands to her face. "Missy Patterson is already teasing me about my hats," she moans through spread fingers.

"Sit down." I lift myself to a half-sitting position against the pillows and pat a spot on the edge of the mattress.

"Mom, I'm a mess."

"We'll go to the mall," I suggest in artificial brightness.

"Mom," she sniffles. "I never should have entered."

"Don't say that," I smile. What am I saying? I think. I am becoming a traitor to myself.

"I don't have a chance," she complains. I put my arms around her then, and pull her close to my chest. Her body, slimmed and toned into perfection, trembles in the circle of my arms. She knows every step of her dance routine by heart—forward and backward. I've financed her spandex and satin wardrobe and five colors of pantyhose on three different credit cards. I'm paying her way at 17½ percent interest.

"Let me wake up," I order. "Then get dressed. We're going shopping."

"You hate to shop," she reminds me. "And shopping for what?" She lifts her downy head from my shoulder. "No more hats," she announces suspiciously. We eye one another for a moment. She's been praying for a miracle, and now I am going to deliver.

"Lady Helena's House of Hair," I confide.

"You don't mean . . . ," she whispers, horrified.

"Yes," I say, "We're going to buy you a wig."

CORINNE DRESSES incognito—blue jeans, Todd's denim jacket, black baseball cap, dark glasses, no makeup. "If anybody sees me, I'll die," she says, hunkered down in the back seat of the car. "Park in back, by the hardware store next to Sears," she commands.

The security guards are just unlocking the doors to the mall at the east end of town when we drive up. "There, park there," Corinne point out, and I pull into a spot near the loading dock of Sears. We sit there in silence, then she says, "Okay, let's go." She opens the car door and makes a break for it. She scans the lot as we pep-step through the double doors near the wig shop, pulling her shoulders forward, tugging the collar of the jacket up around her chin.

Lady Helena's purple-carpeted salon is empty, and we head for a chair near the back of the store. Waves of cool air waft down from the ceiling vents, stirring along with the strains of a violined version of "The Girl from Ipanema." I hum the melody to myself, trying to convey nonchalance. I break into the lyrics. "Tall and tan and young and lovely, the girl from Ipanema goes walking," I lilt with a Latin accent.

From behind her dark glasses, Corinne makes a survey of the store's blind-faced styrofoam forms—some of them flocked with purple and blue velour—all crowned with permanently frozen locks. One whole wall is a display of mounted trophies. The wall across from that is plated with mirrors. Near the entrance, the wall is covered with rows of ribbons and brushes and scarves.

"Now, isn't it a lovely day for shopping?" comes a voice from the door marked "Employees" at the side of the store. Wrapped up in the subterfuge of our sneak attack on the mall, we are surprised by this sudden appearance of a salesperson. And it is Helena herself who is standing there at the door in the wall of mirrors, adorned with a red-henna coiffure. "And what is it you're looking for?" she grins in a row of oversized white caps. Corinne's face goes immediately slack. She does not like the looks of Helena, I can tell. I place my hand on her shoulder and give her a quick reassuring squeeze.

Helena looks from my hand on my daughter's shoulder to my face, quickly sizing up the scene. "First time?" she comforts. "Well, then, let me tell you something," she continues, moving deftly on alarmingly high green heels to our chair. She is perfectly groomed in a two-piece jade suit with pearls. Her shoulders, waist, and hips are all the same width, and the suit fits in a tube from her neck to her knees. Crouching in front of Corinne, she places her ochre-burnished fingertips on Corinne's knees. Corinne doesn't move. Then she sniffles. Then a tear rolls out from under the glasses, and Lady Helena hands her a blue tissue from the box on the counter beside us. "Let me tell you something," she repeats. "Wigs are a fact of life."

I'm a little surprised by the tears. Lady Helena, however, seems well prepared for the event. In looking from chair to chair, I notice the carefully placed boxes of tissue throughout the store. "We're looking for something blond. Natural, of course," I say. Corinne cannot speak in this business of crying and wiping her nose.

"Of course, *natural*," smiles the shop owner. Then she begins a roll call of wigged beauties—"Cher, Madonna, Patti LaBelle, Tina Turner," and looks from Corinne to me. "Take off those glasses," she says to Corinne. "All those gals wear wigs. It's a fact of life."

Corinne is facing us, bare-skinned and pink-eyed. "I'm going to be in a beauty contest," she says.

"Well," grins Helena, squeezing my daughter's knees. "Then we need to make you *feel* beautiful."

TODD'S CREATING sandwiches when we walk in the kitchen. "Where you been?" he asks from the counter, spreading a slide of mayonnaise on each of four slices of bread.

"Shopping," Corinne announces, with a hand to her head, making adjustments, then trailing her fingers to her neck. Todd turns to look at us then.

"You hate to shop," he says to me.

"Oh, it wasn't so bad," I say. "Not this time." I'm looking from Todd to Corinne. She's got two hundred dollars of human hair, not her own, on her head, and he hasn't even noticed.

"The pageant people called," he informs her. "You got practice at two." He stares at her hard. "Hey, that's my jacket," he says. "Don't go wearing my stuff," he warns. "It's not like you don't have enough clothes of your own."

"Todd," I say. "Don't you notice anything about Corinne?"

He turns back to the bread on the counter. "Yeah, she looks better without all the junk on her face. Dede says the only reason for makeup is men." He pastes four slices of waxy mauve bologna to his bread, then stacks two sandwiches on a paper plate.

Corinne gives a great big happy-with-the-world grin to his back. She's passed the first test.

TWO DAYS before the pageant Corinne gets a note in the mail. "I know you're bald. Hope the judges don't find out. Good luck Saturday night!"

Corinne tears the note into tiny pieces.

Dede says it's an act of insecurity on some other contestant's part.

Todd says it's malicious, and he'd expect it out of something as archaic as a meat market show like this.

I say, "There, there." The note is a predictor. Corinne is—to one other contestant, as least—in the running.

THE NIGHT of the pageant, Dede and Todd and I find our places in the city performance hall downtown. We have four second-row orchestra seats, one of which remains empty, due to best-buddy Bess's sudden onset of prepageantry jitters, bringing on what Dede's diagnosed as "sympathetic puking," a symptom of absolute devotion. While Bess had arrived at the apartment an hour prior to our time of departure, we'd had to leave her behind on the living-room sofa with a plastic basin, assuring her that Todd would capture every moment of the night on film, as he'd borrowed Dede's father's video camera.

Dede takes the seat on Todd's left, and I take the one on his right. The hall is packed front to back, and Todd is standing between us, adjusting knobs as he switches on the video camera. "Just because I'm here doesn't mean I approve of this," he says, getting footage of the gilded ceiling work, panning down the fresco of naked gold bodies and cherubs on the wall. "Do I make myself clear?" He is here for Corinne's sake. We all are.

"I know that," I say. "And I do? I approve?"

"Let's just hope the wig stays put," Dede says, and Todd lifts the camera from his eye and stares down at us. For one moment the three of us share an equally mortified expression.

As pageants go, this one is pretty predictable. Todd and Dede spend the first half of the show whispering their own personally based tally of who should win and why into the video-cam microphone. According to Dede, Amanda Dedrickson shouldn't win because everyone knows she cheated on an American history exam, and also because she can't sing, though her efforts at "Don't Rain on My Parade" are valiant, if off-key. Todd aims the camera with determination from contestant to contestant as they appear on stage in their evening gowns. He cuts the power on and off as he films, going for a pastiche effect, broken zippers, Missy Patterson tripping over an electrical cord, painfully displayed cleavage, a musician in the orchestra pit with his finger in his nose.

For the first three acts of the talent competition, I sit stoically applauding in my seat, chagrined at the arbitrary definition of talent. "I cried because I had no shoes," wails contestant number three. "America," Todd reminds us as he aims the camera at the emcee's spats.

Then Corinne takes the stage, and I'm transfixed. The hours of living-room prancing are translated into stage-enlivened wonder. What at home was performed perfunctorily is infused with the adrenaline of the pageant. She enters from stage right in a spotlight, and her spandex glows with pink promise. "Wild thing," the speakers growl from the walls. "I think I love you." I'm counting the steps in my head. She's moving each limb in a perfect mirror image of the other. Leg out, leg in, arm under, arm over. And her hair, that wonder of Lady Helena's, stays put. It should. We shaved her scalp last minute and secured the net with double-faced tape. She moves with the grace of the ballerina she once dreamed of becoming, wide-eyed, smiling to the music. She ends with arms uplifted, victorious. The judges confirm my decision: first place. Todd gets her whole act on film. "Yes!" he whispers urgently in brotherly devotion.

The first half of the pageant is merely a weeding-out process. By intermission, the judges narrow the pool of fifteen contestants down to six, of which Corinne is one. "Are you surprised?" Dede asks right before the second half. The orchestra is warming up, then the lights go down.

"Well, yes," I admit, almost sheepishly. To be honest, I hadn't given much thought to the fact she might win, and I can tell Dede's picked up on this.

"It's okay," she whispers in reassurance, "this whole thing is too weird," patting my knee as the judges take their seats to the left of the stage.

All that remains for the second part of the pageant is the bathing-suit competition and public speaking. "It's showtime," Todd announces, his voice swooping in a menacing prelude. Three spotlights start circling the stage, landing in a center-curtain puddle as the bathing-suit battle begins, and Todd gives an audible groan. The first of the six hopefuls is prancing out on trembling hooves in a red ruffled one-piece. "Clearly an alien life-form," Todd informs the camera's microphone.

"God, everything jiggles," Dede snorts. Todd drops to a crouch at her side. He jiggles the video camera. He turns it upside down. He keeps jiggling it as the red-flounced beauty cavorts. "Todd," Dede hisses, tugging him by his belt back into the seat. Then she laughs.

Two contestants later, Corinne appears on stage, taut, composed, in a tiger-print tank. "Where did she get that suit?" I ask.

"Charged it," Dede smiles. "Of course."

"Of course," I mock. At least it covers her up.

"The judges established new guidelines last week," Dede explains as Corinne takes her place on stage. "In good taste," she winks.

"Right," I say.

Todd films the contestants from the knees down as they maneuver offstage in showgirl style, eyes right and smiling the whole time at the audience. "Mona Lisa," Todd sings into the video cam. "Lady of Spain I adore you," he hams.

"Todd," I half-heartedly scold.

"At which time I hope to work as a lobbyist in our country's capital city," contestant number two beams. "To wake each morning in the city where America's history surrounds us."

"I don't think so," Todd says, "Baby, you'll be flipping burgers downtown, you'll be standing in soup lines. You ain't going nowhere, sister," he sneers, filming Dede's lap.

"Stop," she says. "Just take pictures."

Missy Patterson erupts on stage in a flurry of pink satin. Her shoulders glimmer with sparkling talcum. Her ears glitter in what look like real diamonds. "Where will you be in five years?" ask the judges, and Missy smiles as though collecting her thoughts. In this land of plenty, she will study law and help underprivileged children in the barrio. She is, after all, she reminds us, bilingual.

"Missy Patterson, five to ten for cheating on a history exam," Todd sentences. "Come on, let's see Corinne already."

In a blue silk sheath, Corinne makes my heart stand still. In five years? She will be working as an air traffic controller.

"What?" Todd cries. "I thought it was airline attendant."

"They're somewhat related," Dede defends.

But Corinne isn't finished. She'd like to be located close to her family. In this modern world, she insists, we often neglect the essential value of our families. Ties are broken, we disconnect, we forget where we came from. The judges smile and nod. They like this idea of family. "It is only our sense of family that allows us to belong to this world," she exclaims, then drops softly into her conclusion. "It is only through our families that we eventually find our place."

"Then how come she treats us so bad?" Todd argues. "What's this crap about family?"

"Hush," Dede scolds, and puts a finger to her lips.

"I laugh at your pageant," Todd mocks with the camera aimed dead center of the stage. "I spit on your pageant," he emotes in a thespian baritone.

"Todd, don't you ever stop?" Dede moans, then the audience goes quiet around us.

The judges are nearing a verdict. Missy Patterson, one other girl—a red-head—and Corinne. This is what it comes down to.

Last year's Miss Chidler County emerges on stage, then she makes her final parade along the eye-level runway that's erected down the center of the audience. Todd tries to film up her dress and Dede slaps his hand.

The queen pivots at the end of the runway, rotating her white-gloved hand in perfect, stylized composure, then returns to stand on the stage with the emcee. In the glory of her red velvet robe, she pulls back her shoulders and gives the audience a regal smile. On her lacquered nest of hair sits a twinkling tiara. The three finalists gather in front of her. Todd and Dede go silent. This is it, and we hold our breath.

The three girls huddle close together in finalist camaraderie as the emcee reads off the responsibilities of the new Miss Chidler. As he goes down the list, citing public appearances, parades, speaking engagements, a never-ending calendar of duties, the girls huddle even closer, Missy on one side, the redhead on the other, and Corinne in the middle. Missy, in sisterly affection, puts her arm around Corinne. She holds her close in anticipation, when all of a sudden, the audience gives a collective gasp. My daughter has gone suddenly bald.

Todd jumps up with camera rolling. "That bitch pulled her wig off!" he shouts.

"Is this a joke?" someone says behind us. "Oh, that poor girl."

Corinne stands frozen on stage. The two other girls move back two steps, staring open-mouthed at her condition. The judges are looking at Corinne. She is looking out at the audience, and the audience is looking back.

My eyes are fixed on her face. She has not moved nor stopped smiling. The wig is four feet behind her, but this seems of no concern. Then all hell breaks loose. Corinne grabs Miss Chidler's tiara, ripping if from the head of last year's queen, and she plants it atop her own.

"Wow, that must hurt," Dede says loudly.

"Yes!" Todd is shouting. "Yes!"

Then the orchestra, in some attempt to restore order, breaks into a languid melody while Corinne runs to the end of the stage. The crownless queen is running after her, reaching out for her jeweled headgear. Corinne lets her get just close enough to wrestle the robe from her shoulders. Then Corinne stands there, wrapping the robe around herself with one hand, holding the tiara fast with the other.

"Radical!" Todd cries. "That's my sister," he announces, and the audience stares from the three of us to the stage, back and forth, from Corinne to us. Then Corinne finds our faces and smiles in absolutely radiant control. There has never been a more beautiful queen.

BY SEVEN the next morning Todd's bought the paper, and it's spread out at the foot of my bed. "Bald Beauty Disrupts Pageant," he reads, then holds up the front-page photograph of Corinne in her stolen robe and crown. "Extraordinary," he says. "Like, major extraordinary."

Corinne's snuggled up next to me with a box of doughnut

holes. Last night she ate pizza and chocolate almond ice cream. "Food," she coos beside me. "I love it," she says, placing a brown glazed orb in her mouth. Bess is coming over at ten to bake brownies. Life is returning to normal.

"You're incredible," I say, stretching my toes to the foot of the bed. "You should've taken first place." I rub the top of her warm naked head and she turns to smile at me. She has crumbs in the corners of her mouth.

"Second place is fine," she says. "I would've won, you know," she smiles and reaches for the glass of milk on the nightstand.

"Missy Patterson," Todd says. "What a joke."

"Yeah," Corinne smiles.

"I'm outta here," Todd says as he stands at the foot of the bed. "I need to get more papers. We're supposed to send pictures to Dad." Then his lips spread wide in a boyishly playful smile. "Remember?"

"Oh, God," I groan. Then I laugh.

Corinne laughs too. "Dad's going to die," she says. "Oh, well," she grins.

Todd stops smiling for a moment, and I watch as he studies Corinne's face, meeting her eyes, then lifting his hand to his forehead. "I salute you," he says, conferring admiration the only way he can. Then he's off, turning quickly to leave and thumping down every step of the stairs.

"I'm proud of you for taking this so well," I say, putting my arm around her shoulders. She's down to her last doughnut hole. I rub the top of her head again. "Besides," I say, "it'll grow back."

She holds a wedge of sugared dough in the tips of her fingers and squints her eyes in thought. Then she looks up at me brightly in the quiet room. "I don't know," she says. "I'm kind of starting to like it," she says. "Like this, just like this," she says, putting her hand to her head.

For a moment, by heart flutters side to side in my chest. I sit in absolute silence, then I place my hand over her own atop her head. Her skin is warm beneath my palm, and her scalp stubbles up between the spaces of her fingers. She turns to face me, then, the doughnut hole held one inch from her lips in midair. "What do you think?" she says.

"Well," I breathe out slowly. "Well," I repeat. "I think you'll make the right decision."

She is smiling then, with her arms at my neck, so close I can feel her breath. I could lie there forever with my daughter at my shoulders, as lovely as they come, my naked beauty.

BASTARD CHILD

There is something of my mother in Alice, my wife, though it has very little to do with their looks. My mother was surprisingly pale and small-boned head to toe, yet I'd perceived her as dignified, as opposed to delicate, in light of the fact she'd inherited her father's height, along with her mother's full-bodied flesh and dark Irish curls.

Alice, herself, is tall and slender, but with wide, solid hips and muscled legs, and more angular and taut at those points where my mother rose up into pliant curves. While she also possesses a good measure of Irish blood, she's freckled the length of her body, and has dense auburn hair that lightens two full shades every summer.

At first, I'd been distracted when certain phrases in Alice's voice echoed up from my past, or how the little gestures she made with her hands seemed to perfectly mirror the movements I'd learned as a boy.

Eventually, Alice's similarities to my mother had come to exist as a source of comfort in our married life, as they were part of why I loved her, and were actually more random than I'd first imagined. Maybe once or twice a month, I found myself catching glimpses of some moment from my long-ago life that Alice shared in the present, occurring just regularly enough to be noticeable. Alice has said that she can tell by my silent pensive expression when she's startled up a childhood image and that she's learned that the silence will pass.

Last night, at half past nine, I stood behind Alice at the white chipped-enamel sink in the kitchen. Just beyond the screen above the sink, the red arrow of the windowsill thermometer trembled at the ninety-degree mark. At eight, we'd carried our dishes and plates to the picnic table behind the house, making supper out of cold cuts and potato salad. After we'd finished, our son stripped off his clothes and splashed naked in his blue plastic wading pool beside the table, and now he was asleep in his bedroom above our heads.

As I stood behind Alice in the kitchen, a tomato moth danced along the windowsill, then spread its powdered wings against the screen. "Look," Alice whispered, nodding at the screen. "Odd, how its wings have eyes." She lifted one hand from the sink, pointing out the dark circles on the veiny fabric of its wings. I leaned forward, locking my arms around her waist, resting my forearms on the wide fleshy hill of her hips, my chin on her left shoulder. My bearded cheek rested against her cheek as she dipped the dishes beneath the soapy water, massaging their stoneware surfaces with a net-covered sponge.

Alice's daily encounter with dishes is not like my mother at all. I cannot remember a meal at home with my mother when we didn't first have to scrub off a plate or rinse out a glass, and sometimes we simply didn't bother washing dishes. Mother would look at the pile-up in the sink, knowing there were milk-filmed cereal bowls and glasses with Pepsi candied in the bottom on the end tables in the living room and on her nightstand. Standing in the center of the kitchen, she'd sigh and roll her eyes back so far that there was nothing but a crescent of color left beneath her lashes, and then she'd tell me to get my coat.

We'd start our old Ford truck at the side of the house, and drive down the county line road to the Burger Box, or a mile further, to where the neon red wiener of Hotdog Heaven blinked night and day in its perch above the low, white building. The truck was a noisy, black three-quarter-ton pickup, passed down as a gift from Mother's uncle a month before my birth. While the engine made a furious racket getting started at times, Mother knew just how to coax it to life, working the choke between her fingers as her foot fanned the pedal. Driving into town for supper, fumes and dust filled the cab, rising through the floorboards as we bounced along the gravel roads at dusk. Most often, we ate sitting in the cab, an order of french fries between us on the seat, white cups of catsup balanced on the dashboard.

We laughed and joked about the waitresses or any peculiar sort of person we saw, and sometimes we'd blow the horn when Mother recognized someone from work. I liked it best when it was already dark when we went out. I watched the boys from town in their parents' car, or in cars of their own, passing like schools of fish in and out of the parking lot, girlfriends pressed tight to their right thighs.

As Alice washed the dishes, she shifted her weight from one bare foot to the other. I lifted her auburn hair from the back of her neck, twisted the heavy ropes and curls between my fingers, then pressed my lips to the map of freckled skin at the top of her spine. We had eight years between us, yet I still marveled at the thin spread of skin across the bones of her shoulders, and how, in the center of her back, a line of tiny hairs grew in perfect symmetry on either side of her vertebrae. I licked just lightly there with my eyes closed, tasting the salt and breathing in her sweet and sour smell of summer.

Alice laughed in a gentle warning, saying, "Randall," the way she corrects our son when he is doing something wrong but not quite awful. I reached my hands upward and weighed her breasts through the thin fabric of her cotton T-shirt. Again, "Randall," and then more gently, "Honey, later." That was the same tone my mother used with her boyfriends when they bent down to kiss or stroke her while I was sprawled out in front of them, playing with my checkers or watching television.

MY NATURAL father died when I was two, and the only memories I have of him are ones my mother created for me. I have two small photographs of him, and though there is a strong resemblance between us, I've never been truly curious about his life. Alice complains that I might at least try to find out if I have any brothers or sisters, as she's working on our family tree. The week we were married, we'd driven in from the farmhouse to the county building and obtained a copy of my birth certificate. Alice had been merry the whole morning, yet she'd gone suddenly wild with anger as she examined my papers in the car. "He has a name," she cried out, rattling the paper at my chest.

"He's always had a name," I'd laughed in surprise, keeping my eyes on the road. "It's just not the same as mine," I added, then she pulled the paper back to her lap.

"And he was born in Nogales," she whispered beside me.

"Nogales with an *s*," I echoed defensively, "or Nogalez with a *z*? Which one?" I asked angrily. "Mexico? Texas? Arizona? Take your pick," I ordered a little more gently. "You have a number to choose from."

I looked over at her then as we moved along the highway, and her face was a silhouette against the snow-covered Michigan landscape. "Oh," she said softly, then closed her eyes. "I'm sorry," she added as I slowed for the road leading down to our house, leaning sideways and dropping her head against my shoulder. "Randall, sometimes I react without thinking."

At times Alice softens as we study the two photographs. "It would have been hard not to love him," she smiled sleepily one night late last winter. It was just after midnight, and I'd been clipping my toenails at the end of the bed. I looked up then to where she lay against the pillows, her hair fanning out against the linens. She had lifted the two silver frames from the night stand, and was holding them to her face. "I mean, he's beautiful," she sighed, peering into the frames.

He'd been thirty the year my mother had met him, trucking produce between Florida and Michigan. A few months before she died, she'd come home late one night and found me sleeping belly-down on her bed, the two pictures of my father in my hands. "Hey," she said, "hey," her hand in a jingle of bracelets at my shoulder. "What do we have here?" she laughed, as I rolled over and blinked into the oval of her face. Her body rose from the edge of the bed in a red velvet strapless sheath, and her lips were the color of the dress. She leaned forward then, wobbling on the heels of her black satin evening shoes as she kissed my forehead. Her lips were cool against my skin, and her hair smelled of cigarettes. She rested her cheek against the top of my head for a moment, her breasts scented and close to my face, then she sighed deeply and pulled up straight.

"I found them in your desk," I explained as she held out her hand. She studied the two photographs for a moment, then she lifted her face and met my eyes with a smile.

"Don't look so worried, little man," she laughed. "These belong to you more than me," she said, then she'd placed the photographs side by side in my lap. "Come on, sleepyhead," she said brightly, kicking off her shoes. She tugged me from the bed, ushering me along the hallway, then following behind me down the stairs to the kitchen. It was after two in the morning, and her bare shoulders rippled in a chill as she lit the burners on the stove. "You cold?" she asked as she measured out powdered cocoa and sugar into a saucepan. I yawned and shook my head, then she crossed her arms at her waist, pulling in tight as she shivered.

"There isn't much to tell," she said then as she stood at the stove, making circles in the pan with a wooden spoon. "I was working at that twenty-four-hour diner when he came along one night in the middle of a thunderstorm. The minute I laid eyes on him, I knew something would happen." She went quiet then, staring into the pool of cocoa, then she tossed her hair around her shoulders. "Funny about love," she said softly "When it hits you like that, you can't even stop to think about what's actually happening."

"What did happen?" I asked then, and she twisted at the waist and looked back at me.

"You," she smiled, then turned back to the stove. "You happened," she said, then she paused. "Then he died when you were two."

"How?" I asked quietly, feeling oddly bright and alert.

"In his truck," she answered evenly with her back to me. "Hit a slick spot during a rainstorm. The thing he hated most about driving was storms, rain or ice. They said he died instantly," she added, then turned to face me. "That's the truck in the picture," she explained. "Boy, he loved that truck," she added, then she laughed. "That was some truck, all right. You'd have liked that truck."

In both pictures, he is standing with his right leg angled up into the cab of his truck, a glossy black Peterbilt with glinting chrome. He was tall and slender, evenly muscled and Hispanic, with amazing dark eyes that, as Alice puts it, are "just short of dangerous," and the smiling space between his two front teeth is clearly visible. I wore braces for two years in high school, but I do have his long legs and dark sheaf of hair. I agree with Alice It would have been hard not to love him, and my mother once informed me that there is probably a line of black-haired bastards from here to Florida.

While Alice sometimes softens when she talks about my father, she also says that I have never gotten over being in love with my mother. Alice can wound when she wants to. It's true though, in part, that I never got over Mother's death.

The summer I turned ten, Ed Leeland moved in with the two of us. He was quiet and easy to get along with, as far as I was concerned, but for Mother it was different. To begin with, we started to keep regular hours. Mother had been working nights at the hospital as a nurse's aide, but since Ed worked days as a custodian for the school system, she switched to days. While I missed the freedom of staying up as late as I wanted, I was happier with her home nights. I had stayed alone when she worked the night shift, and even though I knew I could call her at the hospital, I slept better when she was there.

There were other changes too, more subtle, but alarming all the same. Mother had a swinging walk, pushing off the ground with the balls of her feet. Her breasts rose in rounded waves, responding to the movement of her long, slender-boned stride. When I walked beside her, I felt centered by her presence, the steady rhythm of her plump, muscled hip bouncing off my side. It wasn't the twitching bump-and-grind that a stripper makes, but the sensuous sway of a flesh-and-bone metronome. Ed would shake his head, his chin down on his chest, sighing as she pulsed across the parking lot of the hospital when we picked her up from work. "You'd think she was advertising," he'd say, clicking his tongue against his teeth in distress. Eventually the ease of her sensuality began to fade, and she started wearing low-heeled shoes, walking in small measured steps.

Sometimes when I walk with Alice by the Frankfort breakwater, she falls into that same rolling, weaving, elephant-trunk-of-a-walk, and I catch myself seeing her as men must have seen my mother.

There were other, more expected, changes as well, like remembering to close the bathroom door and to hang up my towels after showering. The changes lasted only as long as Ed himself lasted, which was two months shy of three years.

The three of us were sitting at the kitchen table one evening when my mother said simply, "Ed, I've made up my mind, it's time to go."

"You're absolutely certain?" he said, meeting Mother's gaze as she nodded just once in confirmation. Ed was a quiet man, and private. This was the closest to actual quarreling I had heard pass between them firsthand. While they'd both been oddly anxious and quiet around me for the past several months, their arguments were held in whispered anger in the bedroom with the door closed. Ed continued looking at my mother for one long, silent moment, then he stood and walked to the sink. We sat at the table while he dumped out his coffee, running the water after it and rinsing out his cup. "Okay," he said then without looking at us, and he walked upstairs to their room.

This is the only time I remember her washing the dishes. She gathered the glasses and dishes from the living room and piled them on the right side of the rust-stained sink. She squirted dish soap into the noisy rush of the faucets, hot and cold both running full force, flushing up into masses of bubbles. She washed until Ed's car pulled out in a spray of gravel.

I sat at the table and watched as she tilted her head to the left, brushing tears from her cheek with her shoulder. It was so quiet that I could hear the surging engine shift of a semi-truck on the expressway two miles off. Mother took a deep breath, shook her head gently, then exhaled slowly through her nose. "Well," she said softly, turning to me. She stretched herself toward me, her thin arms covered with suds. "Oh, my little man," she whispered into my hair.

"I'm fine," I said, though my voice was higher than usual. We finished the dishes together, then got in the truck and went to Anderson's Cafe for supper. When we left the restaurant, she hung her purse over her arm and pulled me close to her side, leaning on me a little, her hip steadily bumping mine.

That fall Mother started a nursing program through the community college that would lead to her becoming a licensed practical nurse. I was proud that she was attempting school on top of her job, and I helped her study, making flash cards and drilling her on the skeletal system and human anatomy. I tried to help her with chemistry, but it frustrated us both, and she'd fall asleep at the kitchen table as she memorized the symbols on the chart of periodic elements. On the weekends, she practiced making my bed with me in it, or taking my blood pressure until I had red stripes on both arms.

She got all As and Bs, and at the end of the first term in November, we attended a small party for the students and their families. Most of the students in her class had gone into nursing right out of high school, but Mother didn't look much older than any of the others. They exclaimed I looked much too old to be her son. We had punch and cookies in the cafeteria of the hospital after a small ceremony and a speech by the administrator of nursing. We visited with the other students for an hour or so, then right before we left for home, we were introduced to Dr. Andrew Kane.

Dr. Kane wore a plaid Western shirt and jeans under his lab coat, and his hair ran straight back from his forehead in a waxy sheen. He shook my hand, pinching my fingers in his leather palm, slapping my back so it stung. "You know," he said, one eye disappearing in a wink of tan-creased skin, "a hospital can never have enough pretty nurses." Then he took my mother's hand, pulling her slightly toward him in introduction.

We watched television that evening instead of studying, and I had to repeat everything I said to Mother three or four times before she heard me. I wasn't surprised when Dr. Kane began to call her each evening. She answered the phone downstairs, then ran upstairs to take the call in her room, yelling for me to hang up the phone in the kitchen. Sometimes I listened a moment before I hung up and heard him call her "Kitten" or "Sweet Cheeks."

Alice says if anyone should bear guilt over Mother's death, it's Dr. Kane. She says because he was married, he had no right to lead my mother on. I don't see it as clearly as Alice sees it, however. Dr. Kane responded to my mother as many men did. I didn't approve of their affair, but there were many things Mother did beyond reason or convention.

It was during this time that I also began to feel an uncertain awkwardness about my mother. I was enrolled in the eighth grade and finally enjoying forming friendships, as I hadn't had many companions throughout grade school. With each new school year, I'd become increasingly aware that the fact my mother hadn't married my father affected my standing among my classmates. There were parents who had assigned me the status of "bastard child" and some would talk about me within listening range of their children. I was troubled at times in imagining that my classmates were being asked to avoid me, choosing to believe they'd been advised to be kind, even when they hadn't been.

When I look back at my class pictures from first through sixth grade, it is easy enough to recall the precise cruelty certain children exacted, yet I also hold memories of other children who attempted to diminish those blows. While we were aware of the unspoken rules that limited our friendships to the school-yard, there were moments that gave over to joyous and playful abandon, transcending the constraints of my separate reality. Yet in looking back at my grade school photographs, I am reminded more of anguish than gladness, my dark Latino features standing in isolation against the bed of my fair-faced peers.

The junior high, however, took children from six different grade schools. I was among students who had no idea of my background. Still, stories spread, and once the boys in my class saw Mother, it got worse. I took most of the ribbing in the locker room after gym class. "How old was she when you were born? Seven?" If I hadn't been so dark-skinned, they could have seen the blood rise to my face.

When school let out in the afternoon, I'd walk to the hospital and wait for my mother. I liked to sit in the orange fiberglass chairs in the cafeteria and look through my schoolbooks, or draw pictures of World War II bombers shooting lightning bolts of bullets into Japanese boats. When the custodians came humming in with their buffers to do the tile floor, I gathered my books and gym bag and walked down to the lobby. The lobby faced the visitor's parking lot and was filled with groupings of padded chairs and small sofas. Mother always knew where to find me in the lobby, as my favorite spot was at the end of the small gray sofa near the entrance. I'd curl up with my books and watch people come in and out of the big glass doors. If I had money, I went into the gift shop and bought a candy bar or a comic book and chatted with the Red Cross volunteers behind the counter.

One afternoon I was sitting at the end of the sofa doing algebra problems when Dr. Kane walked through the lobby with his wife. He held his hand at her elbow as he led her to the doorway, and I looked away as he bent to kiss her cheek. He kissed her face very slowly, and in a way that seemed too personally tender in the lobby. She closed her eyes for the length of the kiss, then she walked outside, pulling her coat close around her throat. I watched as she walked toward the parking lot, then felt a pull of emotion when she turned, lifting her hand to wave to Dr. Kane, and he was gone. He was bent over the receptionist's desk, a spot that wasn't visible from where his wife stood outside, his voice thrumming in a series of deep chuckles.

When he walked back across the lobby, he glanced up at me, looking momentarily confused, then embarrassed. He lifted his hand to his hair line, then stroked his right temple with his forefinger. He slowed for just a moment and smiled at me briefly with his lips together, then he strode down the hall to the emergency room.

Alice thinks that I exaggerate my mother's appeal, but then Alice only knows her through photographs and what I've told her. She doesn't know the way she moved, the blue veins beneath the white skin of her legs, the way her breasts flattened and flooded her chest when she lay on her back in her bathrobe reading a book on the couch. She doesn't know the voice that imparted helplessness without ever asking for help.

And there are times, looking back, when I wonder how clearly I really saw her. I know that she hid parts of her life from me. When I think about it, though, I am uncertain of what I really heard, how much I felt, or what actually happened.

What I do know is that in December of that year, Dr. Kane stopped calling. It was the only time I remember not having a Christmas tree. Mother worked Christmas Day and left a green foil-wrapped package for me on the kitchen table. Inside was a radio I wanted. I felt guilty that I had asked for something so expensive and actually received it. I spent the day in bed, listening to Christmas carols and road reports. Mother came home after dark and leaned in my door, smiling when she saw the radio balanced on my stomach as I adjusted the dials.

A week later, I was Mother's date for a New Year's Eve party given by friends from work. There was a piano in the living room, and one of the pediatric doctors played from sheet music, calling out, "Everybody sing!" People hung over his shoulder and tried to read the words, spilling drinks on the people next to them. Downstairs was a room for dancing. Mother stood next to me in the darkened room, swaying to the music. Each time she was asked to dance, she would hand me her glass with a napkin stuck to the bottom.

Just before midnight Dr. Kane came downstairs with his wife. For a moment in the shadowy room, Mrs. Kane looked young and pretty. When the lights were turned up at midnight, she seemed to fade beside her husband, pale and sharply thin, a violet stretch of skin below her eyes. Mother was halfway up the stairs when the Kanes moved together to dance. I stood against the wall for a moment before I went upstairs, watching Dr. Kane. His eyes followed Mother up the stairs as he moved against his wife, the square edge of his chin against the top of her head.

I entered the living room right at the stroke of midnight, and everyone pursed their lips for kisses and shouted "Happy New Year!" We left soon after that, walking quickly down the block to where we'd parked the truck. The snow-soft silence of the night was broken only by the cadence of our steps, and Mother said, "Was it this quiet when we got here?" I nodded as I walked beside her, looking up at her beneath the streetlights. She was staring straight ahead, and in the light, her hair billowed in a nest of snowflakes.

Mother died two days later. My aunt came to get me from school, and I knew as soon as I saw her that something was wrong. I rarely saw any of my mother's family, except when my uncle came to work on the truck he'd given us. I went with my aunt to our house, and the yard was filled with cars. In the kitchen, my mother's purse sat on the counter, her gloves and watch placed next to it. I sat at the table for an hour, first staring at the platter of food my aunt had put in front of me, then studying the purse on the counter. Later, when my aunt left the kitchen, I took the purse upstairs to my room.

Mother died at home, hemorrhaging in bed after an abortion. At one point, Dr. Kane came upstairs and took my pulse, then looked in my eyes with a flashlight. He gave me a shot to make me sleep and told me I would feel better when I woke up. He stood at the side of my bed as the shot took effect, and I kept my eyes on his face. "I hate you," I whispered, and then everything went dark.

Alice says I'm morbidly fascinated with my mother. She watches and pretends not to when I take Mother's purse from the top shelf of our closet. Sometimes she'll lean over and say, "Let me smell the handkerchief" or "I want to look, too," as if she wants to understand me. Most often she just leaves me alone with it. There is a wallet, a checkbook, gum still in the wrapper, a date book, aspirin, cough drops, lipstick, a compact of face powder, a handkerchief, a grocery list, and little pieces of trash and paper in the purse. Sometimes I open it and then close it quickly, just checking to make sure everything's there.

TONIGHT, AFTER Alice has finished with the dishes, we went upstairs, and I got the purse down and put it on the bed. I took out the date book and looked at the only entry for the year. On January 2 it says in tiny printed letters, "Dr. Appt. 8 A.M."

I sat on the end of our bed and looked at the other things in the purse. I sat there until Alice sighed and turned off her light and rolled over to sleep; then I put everything back in the bag, snapped it shut and slid it into place on the closet shelf.

I stood at the window of our bedroom and stared out on the night. The wind had picked up and the folds of the white curtains danced up on either side of the sill with each cool thrust. I studied the rounded treetops reaching up against the sky, then I walked across the hall to my son's room. He'd thrown off his sheet, and I stood there looking down on his moonlit four-year-old length. I was going to brush back his hair from his forehead, but I picked him up instead, crushing my face in the sweaty crease of his neck.

A WOMAN LIKE ME

My friend Norman, at fifty, lives in a house made of glass. With ten years seniority, he makes two times my salary. While he's well enough off, he continues to drive a rust-mottled '74 green pickup, and it's parked to the side of the house. I can just see the cab through the door. The truck has a history: five radiators, two marriages.

Every third or fourth year the engine blows when he's pulling the horses. For Norman that's business as usual. Replace the hoses, solder the threatening green-crusted holes, soak the plugs in kerosene, rotate the tires, keep the oil clean. Life, he tells me, is basically maintenance. Life, he pontificates, is a great big car.

Norman is a man of both isolation and routine. He starts drinking each evening at five, sometimes four, not uncommonly at three, most often alone, and once a month he colors his hair and thinks that I simply don't notice.

It is just after six and I'm standing in his kitchen beneath the skylight in a white spray of sun. We have passed the whole day in a kaleidoscopic carousel of shadows and light in Norman's glass house. We have moved from place to place in the drama of the evasive sun and the hot breeze, blaming our summerly distraction and sweat on the voice of the wind at the roof. "Yes," we've agreed. "The wind."

Now the teasing, unsettling gusts and surges have given way to a delicate, cool underbreath, hinting at a July nighttime storm. Here is this house thrusting up on its hill, reaching higher than the trees of the adjacent glacial ridge, in this house where the earth curves downward away from us, we are officially sixty-five minutes into the cocktail hour.

Norman is standing fifteen feet away, between the white linen sofa and loveseat. He's staring out the wall of windows at his daughter's three horses—Lady Godiva, Smartee, Pango-Pango—in the wrinkling green pasture with its mounds of fieldstones. Two miles away the blunt teardrop of an air balloon is dangling above the spine of a hill. Norman's talking to his eldest child, Veronica, one of two daughters, on the cordless. He isn't so much talking as listening, fingering the loose ruddy skin of his neck, pausing every minute or so to pinch the flap under his chin between the calipers of his thumb and forefinger. The dog, Daphne, a small, golden, half-Labrador mix, is positioned on the floor between us. Daphne was assigned to Norman four years ago after his first ex-wife called, six years past their divorce, and said, "Could you watch the girls' dog for a week, just a week?" Today Daphne is lying on her side equidistant between us. She has lived with Norman in his house for four years, and at this moment she is sleeping with her front paws stretched out straight on the carpet of the living room, her hindlegs in a crook on the terra-cotta floor of the kitchen, the metal flooring strip bisecting her middle.

Norman's standing there with a head of variegated hair, talking to his daughter in California, who wants to move out of the dorm and into her boyfriend's fraternity house. "Just for the summer," Norman states, then adds "Right," not as sarcastically as I'm thinking that word, speaking into the white half-shell of phone at his jaw, looking up at me once with a quick, eye-rolling shrug of fatherly exasperation.

Norman thinks I don't know about the secret mixing he does late at night in his house all alone, auburn, ash brown, petroleum jelly at his hairline and around his ears, the plastic bonnet and bobby pins, just thinks I don't notice him showing up at the office with timed applications of color down to his roots every fourth Monday. He wants weird sex in his life. This last is not idle speculation on my part: male, female, group, bondage, leather, lace, rubber, latex, the works. That's what he's confided he longs for at this age, and tearfully sighs that he couldn't possibly handle.

The tearful sighing belongs, he explains, when we talk of these things, to his tortured sense of self. Give me a break, Your Freudian Highness, I sigh. But, no, Barbara Ann, no, he insists. It is that to which he is bound, that which keeps him from jumping between some nubile nymph's thighs. You know, he says, the madonna/whore conflict, an early and damaging repression of his Oedipal lust, an inability to act on impulse without examining all potential pitfalls and pratfalls. Inertia? Complacency? I suggest. No, he scolds, no. At this point in life he wants only friends, he admonishes. My face says I don't believe him. He dates, he defends. And you get dumped, I counter. It's just that he refuses to play human vibrator, he says in an angry complaint. I can relate to that, I tell him, as images of the $69.95 version of Xandria's inflatable woman and her O-shaped mouth flit and wiggle about in my own repressed recesses. Performance anxiety? I remark. Enough, already, he shouts, and I know I've hit that all-time reactive nerve: Impotence! I exclaim. What do you know? he says. What can you possibly know?

Lately Norman's into S and F: Solitude and Fantasy. That stuff is safe. Not like spanking, waking up sore in the morning, ad-libbing explanations to the curious lips at my ear, asking, "Something the matter back there, Barbara Ann? Some reason you can't sit down?" Fantasies won't knock at your door past midnight, saying, "I think we need to talk. Now." Fantasies won't leave love bites and bruises. Mind, this is my friend Norman, not lover, not paramour, not admirer, suitor, main squeeze, steady, not even euphemistic "friend," just someone I know and like, that's Norman, hair dye and all. I'm lying.

I don't drink at all since my father died, and Norman's got his Scotch—a little ice, a little water—constant as a lover and less trouble. Norman's fifty and I'm thirty-two. Sounds like a potential daddy-daughter tryst to me, though my therapist assures me that's not unusual, for a woman like me, considering the facts. I ask my therapist, "You got facts? You call what goes around in my head, what follows me day and night like some noisy obedient caboose, 'facts'? If I needed facts would I be here?" I ask him. "And just what," I continue, "do you mean by 'a woman like me'?"

"At your age."

"At my age."

"All alone."

"All alone."

Young, my father looked like Desi Arnez, back before four years of the Marine Corps sweated off thirty pounds of cherubic fat. By the time I bubbled out a baby-spittled "Da Da," he'd silvered from the temples back, and for one or two years of my toddlerhood, I confused him with Mitch Miller and his bouncing ball on the television set in the family room.

There remains to this day a sense of my father as not being who he was, but reminding friends and family alike of some public figure, or some notable someone else they once knew. Eventually, as his hair feathered white and he took over his family's liquidation business, he was most often mistaken for his own father, a tight-fisted man who'd been dead for years.

He laughed about those cases of mistaken identity as he recounted them to us over six o'clock supper. He laughed, and my mother fluttered in her diet pill dementia, spooning food onto our plates. He laughed. His four children grinned in a silent chorus. He laughed, and our mother stuffed us into silence. "Quiet—Father's home—Please, don't start—you know how he is."

Upstairs in bed with the lights out, we called out room to room, "Why's he think that's so funny?"

"How should I know?"

"What's so funny about looking old?"

"How should I know? Shut up, just shut up."

"He'll hear us."

"He'll get the belt."

"Go to sleep."

"I can't. I'm afraid."

"Don't be afraid."

"I'm not afraid."

"Me neither."

We grinned like a circus audience at his stories, yet I always felt a yank in my gut to think of how he play-acted along with old farmers with crusty hands and blood blisters under their nails. I blushed into fuchsia despair at the sales counter, measuring out gingham and flannel for the church circle women who fluttered and clucked at his side. He faced them in his inherited store over the starched folds of yard goods and stacks of DeeCee overalls with green tags and zippered tobacco pockets, responding, answering, generously inventing replies for a dead man who'd never so much as told his own son he loved him. I have been told by my mother that in his life before I knew him, my father played football, hitch-hiked to California, and swam naked at the gravel pit—so handsome, I become both oddly hopeful and remorseful when I dig through the old photos of him that I keep out of sight, out of mind.

I was born the strange twin of my father, a paradox with a womb. My voice is a throaty-smoked echo of my mother's, so similar that we are often mistaken for each other over the phone; but when I look in the mirror, my father reflects back— wide mouthed, square boned, olive skinned. My eyes are his, and belonged to his mother before him, glistening and dark, an effort to tell pupil from iris. His body lies in the family plot at the north end of town, and I go there for conversation. It's possible to bury a drunk.

Back to Norman. Slim, short, nervous, and smart little guy, thinks he's an ugly duckling, thinks he knows everything. I tell him he's got terrific hair, and he does, a great thick shelf falling back on his neck, thinning in front, its true color an ambiguity, big glasses below his forehead, and genuinely green eyes, like you hardly ever see in this day of tinted contacts. He's off the phone, and we're looking at the glossies for an advertising blitz we've commissioned for our boss-hog Geoffery—"don't call me Jeff, damn-it-all"—DhuVarren. The photos span the kitchen counter edge to edge in Norman's vaulted "great room," a glassed-in tank of isolation that was built when Norman, after forty, experienced divorce number two. The whole house is an announcement, angles of cedar and mirrors and blond carpet, and the one-bedroom loft an intentional act of sensory deprivation, a subliminal "Don't touch me," whispering down from the ceiling beams.

We're standing there, and Norman says, "Jesus." Geoffery left a few minutes ago down the quarter-mile dirt drive, summer dust rolling in a cumulus at the bumper of his 280Z, racing to pick up his date for the evening, Belinda from systems design. She is his latest trophy, an odd tower of flesh from MIT: large, loose, round shoulders, and deep pores, not at all Geoffery's usual mantelpiece. Geoffery himself is a blond Dutch-boy from Grand Rapids, middle-aged swell of a belly under his Pierre Cardin blazer, shelves of flesh at his shoulders, gold curls of hair at his forty-nigh-fifty-year-old neckline, and, in reference to Belinda, has said only, "Baby, it's her mouth." Of course, since he's said that, Norman and I have made a careful study of her lips, full slices of Taffy Apple, framed in a penciled line of Estée Lauder. I bet I know where they've been.

Norman goes "Jesus," again. We're there in his house in the middle of the Michigan landscape, the three horses now loping down the hill to the north, in this house made of glass and just enough wood to support it, even a circular window over the tub so you can look from the solarium into the bath and see whoever is covered with soap from the waist up. Norman says he goes around naked since his daughters aren't staying with him, because of the erotic appeal. Me, I think naked is good only because half the time I'm running late and need to trot bare-assed down to the basement for clean underwear or to iron a blouse, but the erotic stuff, well, I have "issues."

Norman goes "Jesus," and I know why. It's a little past seven, and this deal with the Midwest's most popular group health insurance plan is closing in. The "Jesus" is not from the deadline, but because of the glossies we're thinking about using, and that's what has put him on edge, that's what's made him splash more Scotch in his glass. I write copy. I don't deal with getting the image right, I just have to find the words for Norman's layout. I'm terrific at planting suggestions. Give me an image, I'll take it the distance. For instance, this deal with Arms and Arms Insurers out of Chicago was a cinch: Two strong arms in the night. Took about three seconds to get it right, and Geoffery's said it's a go. He's chosen models with well-defined biceps, sanded elbows, slender wrists, good manicures, Rolexes, Movados. Advertising: if I could do with my body what I do with language, I'd have slept with half the country. Not that I'd want to. It's the part about getting undressed I don't like, especially with strangers.

Norman's standing there with the light from the stained-glass fruit and vine hanging lamp making a church of his forehead. He's got this "Jesus" suspended in the air, and I'm not talking for all the thoughts going off in my head. Mostly I'm a locked box these days. Maybe I like running around the house all alone in the nude, but put me next to another human being, and we're talking two layers of clothing. Summer or winter. Here's how it goes. Two shirts—a man's T-shirt under a cotton blouse, a commonsense bra, regular cotton panties, then a lycra brief for support, jeans, socks, or maybe a long skirt, and in that case, a slip, and over all this, day job or night work, a company smock: white with three red As on the breast pocket—"Advertiser's Art Associated."

Norman jokes. He calls us "Artsy-Fartsy Asshole Anglers." Sounds like sodomy to me. Speaking of which, these glossies are what sent him into his "Jesus" state, the Lord's name in vain whistling through his nose with a hostility the likes of which I have not heard since the time my next-to-last ex-lover, at that time female, found me with my arms around our accountant, male. But maybe the night in that club in Savannah rivals that, what with two hormonally enraged Thirty-second Rangers from the local post coming in with smoke bombs and camouflage face paint, queer bashing. "Damn lesbians," they screamed, right before flushing us out with red smoke.

Norman thinks life has passed him by. Passed him by, as in no chance for, no hope of, give me another Scotch. His nose-whistling hostility comes out of the models we have here in front of us, pouting, posturing, pseudo-anguishing, trying to portray sick people in a hospital, and not one of them looking ill. Norman, now, he's a little pale, maybe a subtle scoliotic bent to him, but he's here in the flesh, looking at these beautiful bodies, thinking, "Jesus." But as well as I know him, right down to his second ex-wife's favorite position—from behind and hard—I can't get a handle on his feelings. So I ask, "Do you want to be them, or have them?" Meaning the models, of whom even the ones from the over-forty pool look better than I did at twenty, let alone today, let alone Norman at fifty. But, me, I'm a sucker for a good mind. Intellect. Someone to talk to after what it is I think Norman is pissing and moaning about not getting enough of.

So he finally answers, lighting his 141st cigarette of the past four days. He's on pack number eight. I count. He goes, "I just want a little of what they have, babe." Babe. He's been calling me this for a couple weeks, out of what I don't know. "It's unfair." He's whining now, so I smile. I smile this great big all-my-teeth-showing smile, and laugh. I like when he whines. It's honest petulance. "If the world were fair, this stuff would be evenly distributed. I'd be four inches taller, you'd quit obsessing about body image, and these people would suffer more with ideas of average."

"You're not average," I tell him. "I don't waste my time on average. Average is inexcusable." He stands there beside me running his fingers over the glossies, then back through his wonderful mess of hair, then he slaps his palms on the glossies, and settles down a bit, suckling on Scotch.

Sometimes I feel like we're married. Six years, that's how long we've shared the wall between our desks at the office. I hired in right after Connie, ex number two, left him. When he gets smashed he tells me she was the best sex he ever had. And I ask him to tell me what kind of marriage that makes for, other than in the bedroom. Marriage, I tell him, takes up the whole damn house. And he tells me it's different for men, how when the night comes in through the skylight he lies awake until two or three thinking about the blue of the moon on her skin. That's different? I ask. From what? Seems very poetic to me, Your Great Sensitive Highness, I tell him. Seems very lovely and sad, though a bit wasted after seven years of divorce. Of course I don't like this Connie, though I never met her. I have learned to hate here in absentia.

So I tell him, "Well, maybe it is evenly distributed. We just got our share pasted on the inside." He doesn't like this explanation. He spills some more Scotch into his tumbler, and lifts the wiry antennae of his brows. I don't think those get dyed, but I wonder. So we're standing there, with him thinking I'm trying to placate him, but I really do love his insides, and I tell him that. But he's not buying it, not a word, and I'm getting fed up, because three years ago I got kind of hot for this guy, for the stuff in his head, and if he's going to shake off what I value, then what's anything matter? He's pulling real hard on a cigarette, trying to kill himself. I smoke a little, a puff here, a pack every week or so, but not like Norman. So maybe I let myself fall for him, maybe he'll croak. Maybe someday he'll drive drunk into a tree. On purpose. Overdose. Take a window. I don't know, but lately it's hard to be close without wanting him closer. And now he's gone all sour over these primped and powdered models, male and female alike, and me, what am I, a slab of genderless salmon?

"Look at me," I say. The sun's ended up in a somersault on the hill outside his glass house. He takes another passionate drag on his smoke and looks at me, just barely. He does that, looks to the side, not at you.

"It's you and me, babe." He works his lips around the butt, real old-movie-star-like. Once, half-crocked, he told me he was a virgin until almost thirty. He never said if he got laid before wife number one, but my guess is no. So he told me he's missed out on ten years minimum of good sex, since most guys start poking around at eighteen or nineteen. That kind of talk gets me crazy. It's like he's just waiting it out, no nothing, just bitching and drinking, waiting to die. I could give him ten years in a month. Or less.

"It's not 'you and me, babe,' for shit," I say. "I'm not soaking up Scotch. I'm standing here making a living. I'm standing here. You're standing there. There's this little bit of physical space between us. The sun is sitting out there on your fucking hill. You got a house so far from the road you can run around naked and nobody sees you. Your daughters come to visit whenever you want, and they love you. Give me a break." I say. "Give me a cigarette," I command. I'm really crazy at this point. "Light it for me, fathead."

My father used to go on binges and then sober up for a week or two. Later, he learned to drink so it didn't show. When I was fifteen, my mother started sleeping on a twin bed pushed up against the wall of their room. My dad bought the bed himself, paid cash and had it delivered. Two years later I moved out and played musical mattresses in my dorm room. Now that my father is gone, I visit with my mother at night over tea at her kitchen table, and we try to untangle the past. Every so often she tells me more than I ask for, like how she should have run off and married Eddie Fontane, like he wanted. Her face went pink when she confided she'd dated him the entire time my dad was away at college, even necking on the sofa when her parents weren't home. He'd been wild about her, crying like a kid when she turned him down. Now she thinks about him off and on, wondering what kept her from marrying the boy she knew loved her, ending up instead with the one who kept her guessing. She doesn't ask much about my personal life. What she hears doesn't make her happy. She's got four kids, and she laughs that all counted, she's been to seven of their weddings. I tell her that eventually we'll get it right. Sometimes I fall for women, and sometimes I fall for men. But never for long. For the most part, I've learned how to like being alone. I don't know what I want, but it's starting to fill up my head, and it's here in this space between us in Norman's glass house.

"Do you think we should be lovers?" Norman says through a jet stream of cigarette smoke, and I go all cold in the face and my knees are a little loose, like maybe I should sit down. Six years, I'm thinking, and finally this guy's catching on. But then

I think maybe he's just going for shock. Maybe he's trying out some weird fantasy resolution. These artists. You never know.

"You think sex will do it for you?" I say, and I sound kind of bitchy. So I add, gently, "Is that it?"

"No," he says, no smile, no smirk, no anger. "No. I think it could wreck things. I think it could screw up our working together. I think of how messy it would be, and I stop thinking about it at all. It could get us in trouble. I don't like trouble."

And then I go "Jesus." I reach for his glass, pick it up and take a mouthful of Scotch, and he lifts his head in a spastic flinch. I put the glass down hard and go, "Jesus. Jesus, fucking Jesus, fucking Jesus Christ," and he finally laughs, like he laughs when it's really funny, and so do I. The whole room shifts as the sun tumbles down past the skyline, falling beneath the curve of the earth so what's left of the day is coming up from under us. The corners and ceiling fill with shadows. There's about two inches between us now. I could reach out and touch him, but I never touch anyone on purpose. So I stare at his hands. They're wide and broad, not at all like the rest of him. I stare at his hands, the palm curled around the arc of his glass again where I set it down, the cigarette at his lips in his fingertips.

"Mostly, I just like kissing," I say.

"Kissing," he echoes.

"And talking in between the actual kiss, and sometimes during," I smile, but not at him. We're not looking at one another, not even from the side.

"And talking," he says, "We've got some weird rhythm going. I could say anything, and he'd repeat it. We're dancing in a mirror of words. Then he uncurls his fingers from his glass and moves them along the edge of the counter. He moves them next to my hand and he touches the tip of my thumb. This is all of me that he touches. It's a game of tag.

I close my eyes for a moment. I've been dreaming too much the past year, and I'm tired of dreaming and not knowing why. Mostly I dream of my father. When he died, I took the pillows from his bed, and now I use them on my own. Sometimes I dream about Norman. I dream about sitting beside him in his old beat-up truck, going nowhere real slow, being lost and not minding. Once in a dream we were riding his daughters' horses, bareback, going downhill, sliding into sand, in color.

"I dream about you," I say then. I've never told him this before. And then he gets quiet, more quiet than the quiet before. We are standing in Norman's glass house. In the silence between us I can hear him breathing. I can feel him breathing, because that's how it goes with a woman like me—lips, breath, teeth, the weight of his hands in my hair.

NECESSARY DISTANCE

A couple months back, I'd started watching what I said about Gene to my mother, even though there hadn't been much to say at that point. And while there still wasn't much to talk about, she didn't have any qualms about bringing up his name. She worked the topic of Gene into our chitchat through leading questions or in the guise of an afterthought, saying "Is that old truck of Gene's still running?" or "I suppose you'll be eating supper with Gene."

More often than not, I could predict her line of inquiry, or at least figure out in which direction she was trying to lead me. Yet during one of those rare moments when I'd allowed her to discuss Gene at all, I'd been surprised to hear her referring to him as "undereducated." I was even more surprised by how quickly I demanded an explanation. "What's that supposed to mean?" I asked, irritated that I'd taken the bait.

"Undereducated," she clarified with a smile, "As opposed to uneducated," and she insisted he was full of promise, especially in light of my hiatus from dating. "Rebecca, after all's said and done," she encouraged, "what does it matter at Gene's age that he's started going just a wee bit bald, and he's so tall, why, a person barely notices what's on top." Being tall was at the top of her list of qualifying characteristics for men, following the requisite university degree: height, money, hair, good hygiene, in that order, with bonus points for men who presented a dark-eyed and black-haired Latino appearance, sometimes extending to well-defined Italian features and olive skin.

As for me, I've learned to value tender hearts. He had one, I told her, but my mother and I clearly barter in different markets. "Now, a strong heart," she stated when I was still stuck between deciding about seeing Gene at all. "A strong heart," she'd repeated. "Now that's something even I'd like to run into."

WITH GENE at the wheel of my new blue car, we rolled tight in the outside lane of fast-moving Memorial Day traffic. It was just after four, and we were headed home at sixty-five miles per hour. Through the passenger seat window, the welts of Michigan hills folded into the near-rain horizon. Along the hilltops, the pines and firs seemed to finger the slate-bottomed distant clouds. I could tell Gene had turned to look at me then, taking his eyes off the highway just briefly, his voice coming at me in a sideways chuckle. "I don't know about you," he said. "You have this way of looking at the world and seeing ten times what other people see." Then he paused for a moment before adding, "And maybe ten times more than you need to see at all."

This was something people have been telling me all my life, especially my mother. "Rebecca," she lectured, "at least try to give the impression that you're listening, even if you're not." And while my tendency to get swallowed up by my thoughts was clear early on, my mother eventually learned that I always picked up everything going on around me. The year I finished high school, six months early and with English honors, I ranked fourth in a class of 327, and my mother laughed about this to her friends. "It's a mystery to me how she did it," she said, "what with her head stuck in the clouds all the time. Sometimes I have to clap my hands right in front of her face just to get her to answer a simple question."

Even though my mother had laughed about me to her friends back then, she'd always been serious about lecturing her children, a habit that hadn't ended, by any means, when each of us left home. And while most of her lectures, however tiresome, were made in my direction, at times her intentions weren't clear. The year I started teaching, for example, I was home for a weekend visit, and I imagined she was working up to another sermon about how I should dress for my new job. "I was reading this article about how people make up their minds on the basis of first impressions," she started out as we stood at the kitchen counter. "Ten seconds," she announced brightly, spooning dough onto a cookie sheet. "It says people decide if you're right or wrong in the first ten seconds."

I turned to her and shrugged. "Right or wrong for what?" I asked. "Do you mean employers, or just people in general?"

"Well, the article was about how to sell real estate," she explained, "how to size up potential buyers, which people it makes sense to spend the most time on." She was quiet for a moment, then she said, "But you can apply the idea to all kinds of situations. And to buyers and sellers both, you know." At that point I only nodded. "It's not just the way you dress," she continued, and that threw me for a loop, since I'd been waiting for her bit about the virtues of classic navy blue jackets and A-line skirts. "Rebecca," she said, "maybe you could practice looking pleasant," then she hesitated. "Around the other teachers, I mean, and for your students, you know," and I shook my head in disbelief. "No, listen," she urged, "you just seem so standoffish. Maybe your students wouldn't be so afraid to approach you."

"Mother," I said carefully, "my students aren't afraid of me, they like me." I made an effort to speak slowly. If I didn't, she'd start scolding me for sounding angry. "My students come right up to me and ask any old question they want," I told her. And then as I stood there in silence, a thought tumbled clumsily into place. "Mom," I said quietly, "are *you* afraid of me? Is that it?"

"No," she answered, and just a beat too quickly. "Afraid of my own daughter?" she laughed with a toss of her head.

"I can't believe this," I said gently. Her cheeks had turned pink. Her forehead was pink. "My mother's afraid of me," I teased softly in a little girl's voice, hoping she'd look up and meet my gaze.

"I'm afraid of where you go off to," she sighed then, staring down at the cookie sheet. "You get so serious sometimes, so distant, it's like you're a hundred miles away," she explained. Then she finally looked up and turned her face toward mine. "And when that happens," she whispered, "I'm still here, and you're not."

In the car with Gene, I remembered how easily my mother

had allowed me to put my arms around her that afternoon in her kitchen. I pulled her close and she hadn't pulled away. And when I'd whispered at her ear, "I'll try to smile more, Mom," she hadn't said a word, she'd just hugged me a little tighter.

"Hey," I said, turning toward Gene, and he lifted his eyebrows. "Do I look grouchy to you?" I asked, and he shot me a curious grin, one quick twist of his neck, then he went back to looking at the road again. "I just wondered," I smiled. Gene's hand passed an inch from my knee as he punched the cigarette lighter in the dashboard ashtray. He smoked a pack a day, sometimes less. Other than Gene, I never let anyone smoke in my car. He didn't touch me as he lifted the circle of ember to his face. He never touched me during the day, since the kids were always right there in the middle of things. But in a way, I liked the feeling that came with all that, at least for then.

I HAD a ten-year-old son named Tad, born big and plum faced and bawling, who, at ten, remained exuberantly large and exhibited the spiked-thatch genetic force of his father's hair. Gene had a ten-year-old daughter named Erica, and Derek, a nine-year-old son. The three of them sat in a row behind us, elbow to elbow, a prepubescent clutch of lips and limbs, hinting, from time to time, of the unavoidable grief they would someday cause us. Gene and I often discussed, late into the dark, our future sad roles of letting go, and how there were already inklings of what lay ahead: Erica's ardent interest in glossy teen posters of shirtless boys without facial hair; Tad's insistent finger at his chin, pressing at his newly blossomed lone pimple; Derek's lingering glance down the front of my swimsuit at the beach.

"I'm an old lady," I'd chided. "Look at someone your own age, already."

"You've been busted," his father punned right away, quick in making light of Derek's red-faced curiosity. Later, Gene put his hand where his son, only somewhat less shyly, had peered just a few hours earlier. "Can you blame him?" he'd asked, in the half-serious way he had of acting helpless each time he started to touch me. I couldn't quite figure out why he joked around like that, but I imagined it was tied to how his marriage had broken up, and something I might do better to never understand.

As the air threaded through the car, every so often I caught a whiff of the kids. They all needed baths. We'd intended on one final noon swim to bring them home clean, but we'd been distracted midmorning by a racket behind the cabin as something made its way along the rise leading up from the marsh. Gene teased the kids, saying, "It's a bear, sure enough, so we'd better get to loading the gun."

"A gun?" Tad shouted, sounding too happily alarmed. I shook my head. There hadn't been a gun in the cabin for years.

"Nope," I corrected, speaking firmly in Gene's direction, "no gun."

"But what about the bears?" Gene smiled as our eyes met. Then he winked and turned away, going on to describe in great detail how bears liked to mutilate their prey before eating it. "They're especially fond of devouring folks limb by limb," he finished up, at which point Erica raced back into the cabin. She was crying in the bottom bunk when I found her, and it took thirty minutes to convince her that her dad was only kidding.

By the time Erica and I reemerged from the cabin, a large gray turtle with a square welted shell had cleared the top of the rise, revealing itself as the source of the noise. Even with the five of us standing there around her, the turtle moved slowly through the clearing. We followed, trailing her back to a ledge of pale limestone. She'd come up from the edge of the marsh to lay her eggs at the edge of the rock, and we spent four hours watching her digging up the earth and thrusting forward and back.

And now the moons of the kids' toenails and fingernails were wedged with the residue of riverbank digging and campfire prodding. They were sitting tangled behind us, suckling at the forty-four-ounce malteds we'd bought at the Dairy Bar in Cadillac. They were happy enough dirty, and with their cheeks sunk into hollows in drawing up chocolate through their straws.

Erica was particularly adept at making duck calls by dragging her straw in and out of the hole in the plastic lid. Her father, at that moment, on the brink of exasperation, said quietly, "Erica, stop." This I considered true parental divinity. My father, in similar car-bound situations, believed in communal discipline, reaching behind him to blindly slap any available child's bare thigh. Erica, placidly fearless, continued with her quacking, until Gene, lifting his eyes to the rearview mirror, met her gaze and informed her that if she did not stop with the noise, she'd have no lips left in which to place the straw. And finally, at this warning, she chose to cease and desist.

Derek, on the far left beside her, was studying baseball cards held close to his face, lifting them under the bill of his New York Mets cap. Every once in a while he exclaimed, "Hey, Dad," and read off extraordinary batting averages or R.B.I.s in his boyish soprano, and his father answered, "Amazing, isn't it?" and meant it. The two of them played catch every evening, tossing radio announcer game talk between them in the violet night air. They lobbed the ball curb to curb across the quiet, oak-lined street, where they lived in the yellow clapboard house that Gene's mother had bought and rented to them. The nights they played ball, I sat in the porch swing and watched them.

Erica, seated between the boys as the keeper of peace, was leaning against Tad in her "Maybe I'll be your girlfriend, maybe not," sort of way. They were reading comics. The same age by a month, that's how it went with them, hot and cold, in their loves-me-loves-me-not preteen banter. Last summer with Tad had been simpler, his spats with the neighborhood girls ending in, "Well, then you can't come to my birthday party, so there." Now he laughed at the words *nuts* and *balls*, and Erica had confided in an Amoco bathroom that she'd die if she didn't get a bra before school started again, "just die." She wanted to take dance lessons in the fall, jazz and tap, if they could afford it. If I could have looked like someone else at ten, though God knows who'd want to be ten again, I would have wanted to look like her. She had a ponylike fit of blond hair and skin that went instantly gold in the summer, not that red and peeling mess most of us have to deal with, but honest California-girl eighteen carat. She was as tall as Tad, but not thick like him. He'd hit one-twenty that summer, and she was ninety, if that, so small around she was always hammering new holes into her belt and cinching it tighter. I hoped she got to take dancing lessons, because she was as limber as an art eraser, even though Gene complained that she was a "remarkably graceless child." Every time he said that, I scolded, "Don't tease."

A few minutes after Gene convinced Erica to stop making noise, I felt her tipping forward between the front seats. The straw was caught in the suction of her lips, and I knew she was hoping to catch the drop of a phrase, a quick breath of laughter, the touch of a wrist, anything. She lifted her pale brows when I finally caught her eye, feigning surprise, and then smiled chocolate malted at me. She listened with a ten-year-old's curiosity. She listened with a child-of-divorce interest. We were listening to ourselves as well.

THAT LATE afternoon sailing home in the car, I gave Gene an analogy. Maybe he liked it, and maybe he didn't. I teach freshman English at a big university, and he's working on his secondary-ed degree at the state college back home. He'd said maybe he'd teach English too, but it was hard to tell if he meant it. Conversation fell between passing silences for us those days. We waited to see what the other one said, while thinking—before saying—what might make too much of a serious difference. We used comparisons and metaphors when we talked about ourselves, and only by use of example, making studied references to our pasts, our ex-spouses, our children, but not about us, not about the here and now. We didn't make direct connections, because it might kill us to say what we felt. Those were the silences I sensed, guarded and roaming the separate histories between us. We both knew all we'd ever need to know about busted hearts.

Sometimes in the night, Gene almost got me to talk. When he pressed his lips to the pulse at my neck, I whispered, "Oh, Gene," as he kissed at the dip of my throat. And then he went, "Oh, Gene, what?" with genuine playful interest, so that I almost believed he was asking me to say it, wishing me into saying it. He held me away from him once, gently, and I almost gave in.

It took just a minute for my head to clear and my heart to pull guard duty. I said, "Stuff, it's just stuff. It's nothing," and kissed my way out of it. I had three years of French in high school. I translated the entire original monk-printed Beowulf manuscript my first year of graduate school. I could have said it in another language, but I couldn't say it in English. When I stared at him in that wordless distance between us, sharing the breath off his lips, he pulled me to him like I'd been lost, and he'd only just then found me.

THESE WERE the things my ex-husband had said in the course of our two-year marriage:

"You're the best."

"Get your fat ass out of my life."

"Never leave me."

"Nobody else would want you."

"I want to die in your arms."

"Idiot fat-girl, go home to mother."

Sometimes, too drunk or wired to put a complete string of words together in a thought, he left it at "Idiot. Idiot."

He said these things in between affairs with party store clerks, enlisted women, topless dancers with tattoos of tigers and swords down their thighs. He said these things during and after and in between the rutting and alcohol, then he'd come back to me in a flux of repentance. After a while I stopped listening. After a while I was glad when he didn't come home. That's what happens when you're blasted apart too many times to keep track of. You drop your heart off at the side of the road, like some pregnant stray you never should have fed to begin with.

MY FATHER had been dead almost three years, and I'd had a premonition two years before they found the tumor. I was driving home from graduate school with Tad strapped in beside me in our twelve-year-old car that only sometimes ran two entire weeks without breaking down again. It was an icy December day, and the car skated along the two-lane highway toward the center of Michigan. Ten miles outside of Lansing the vision hit me: I was sitting in a pew of my childhood church, and my father had died. I'd dismissed it, thinking it to be triggered by the drive home, by the holidays, by the loneliness of raising my son through the unending hours of graduate work. But that was almost six years ago, before I learned to believe in the two of us, Tad and me.

IN MY bed alone at night in our apartment, there are times when my drifting into sleep dredges up echoed-back memories of my father's rich tenor, startling me awake until dawn. My mind insists on preserving the rolling sound of my name in his voice, that rising, three-noted, stern rendering of his "Rebecca," the playful teasing of his "Becky-Anne," which he himself had carried over into my life, long past childhood. These are uneasy, unasked-for memories, and though my friends have assured me they'll eventually pass, every few months his voice rises up at the edge of my sleep.

At times, I assign the source of his dream voice to the fact he'd called my name as he died in his bed, which is something I hadn't liked finding out. The morning he died, I was 128 miles south, in front of my first class as a full-time instructor. He told me himself that was where I belonged, whispering, "Go on, now," as I bent to kiss his face that last time. I'd produced the only grandchild of our family at that point, and my son's joyous presence allowed my father and me the only chance we'd ever have to finally turn to each other as friends. Tad had been a month shy of one when I admitted the mistake of my marriage by returning home. My father's reluctance over taking us in was short lived once his house was filled stem to stern with my son's gleeful and noisy existence. He adored Tad without measure, in a way he'd never been able to openly love his own children.

My sister was the one to inform me that he'd asked for me right up to his final drugged sleep. And even though I'm certain she knew that what she'd told me would stick like a hook in my gut, I came to forgive her. She held our father in her arms while he called my name, and she didn't let go.

THE LAST time Tad's father took our son for a weekend visit was seven years back. When Tad had an accident in his pants, his father broke Tad's potty chair against the bathroom wall. He rubbed the soiled terrycloth under Tad's nose, saying, "My dog has more sense than you." After that, he'd held Tad's head between his hands and forced his face into the toilet.

I'm not sure of all the other details, exactly, but that's what my ex-husband's third ex-wife Tina had told me, seven years after the fact, seven years after she should have informed me. Tad still had accidents. I still had court orders for total custody.

MY EX-HUSBAND was on marriage number four, his history of wedlock beginning at age eighteen. His first wife was fifteen when they married, and she already had a daughter by somebody else when she met him, a blond-haired, slender child, with little white-chip teeth and loose limbs. Her name was Tamara Elizabeth April Reed Marsey, a stretch of names that held her roped to the worlds of her parents' pasts. I started calling her T.E., and after a while, so did everyone else. She was the flower girl at our wedding, shivering down the aisle in a pink-chiffon party dress one January afternoon in the Methodist church downtown. My ex-husband's mother sat in the back of the chapel holding her newest grandchild, his seven-month-old daughter who was born to his ex-wife three months after we met. I missed seeing the girls when I left him, and still did. T.E. had been nabbed twice for shoplifting last year. If she did it again, she'd get locked up in the county home. That's what she told me on the phone last winter, and she'd sounded half-proud about the fact something terrible might happen to her.

The day we'd stood in front of the minister, I started laughing in the middle of the ceremony. At the very last minute, I realized I didn't love the guy, though my mother attributed my giggling fit to nerves, and shrugged it off as she slipped me two ten-milligram Valiums.

I lived with him in Georgia for two years, at the edge of the woods where our trailer backed up on a still. Moonshining was traditional business down there, and the men who ran the still were all somehow related to the sheriff of our little town twenty miles from the army post. There were families living back in the woods, down to the river, in shacks and old trailers, and they were all related to one another. They kept dogs to protect the stills. Those dogs weren't pets. They were half-wild, kept around to drive away curious strangers and alligators coming up from the swamp. The dogs slept in old crates and half barrels. Some were tied up and some were chained and some ran loose. To keep them mean, the men beat them, in front of their wives, in front of their children. Sometimes the dogs killed one another, battling over the rare hamhock or slop flung out into the yards. When we drove back to our trailer late at night, the dogs flinched when our headlights lit the woods. They would lift up from sleeping and break into howls before they were fully awake, pulling forward to the ends of their chains, their hair in ridges against the bony crests of their spines. They'd expected the worst at all times.

I'D BEEN all set to talk to Gene about birth control, since I was thirty-four, and I'd even practiced out loud in perfecting just the right tone of nonchalance for bringing up the topic. Gene himself was a year older than me, and I'd been confident that he'd accept it as fact how people our age simply needed to talk about how all that stuff worked, as to get it out of the way.

Yet I felt the world tilting up for a moment in the middle of washing our first night's worth of dishes, when, having fallen into a detailed discussion of the surgeries that had followed Tad's prolonged birth, Gene informed me he'd had a vasectomy. In the context of what we'd been discussing, it was actually rather clever how he'd worked in this bit of vital information, yet it hit me off guard, and so oddly quick, I actually felt faint for a minute or two. I'd been celibate for nine years at that point, but it was one thing to focus on prophylactics. It was another thing altogether to have to start thinking of turning to Gene with nothing between us but air. It could have ended up meaning something more than I'd wanted it to.

"It was a medical necessity," Gene confided as I'd stood there in silence at the sink, and saying it with absolute conviction, due to the history of his ex-wife's affairs, but I hadn't liked how the learning of this fact started playing out in my head like a movie. The whole thing had taken place so far back, I knew in all truth that it should have meant nothing at all, just the slice of a scalpel and a couple stitches, and mocking the fact I'd bought a box of condoms at the drugstore two weeks in advance. They were sitting at the bottom of my overnight bag in the bathroom, right next to the tube of spermicidal foam I'd picked up ten days later. Part of the reason I'd added in the foam came from what I knew about double protection, but it had been equally due to my surprise in finding it was now part of IGA's regular stock, and right there at the end aisle, beneath the sign reading "Feminine Products." I'd gone ahead and figured out the logistics of birth control methods, but instead I ended up with Gene's life playing out in my head, unrolling the rest of that evening in an endless flickering film of scenes from his past, and relentless in how I kept the plot and action moving forward nonstop.

Our first night in the cabin, I left all my clothes on, saying I'd taken on a chill, shivering out my excuses for not changing into my pajamas, even though the kids had pulled theirs on just prior to making s'mores and fighting over who'd get which bunk. After they settled down in their sleeping bags, Gene kept the fire going so steadily I could feel the heat sinking as deep as my bones. All the same, I took off my sweater, nothing else, and then only because Gene had said, "Aren't you a bit warm, there?" since I kept wiping at the sweat along my hair line.

Even with both of us still dressed in our jeans and T-shirts, we cuddled and kissed on the couch near the fire, from just after midnight until the sun started coming up and casting violet shadows across the room through the windows. At some point past three, I ended up straddling his lap with my thighs, which he hadn't expected, and at first made him laugh, then later brought a little moan up from his chest as I pressed myself tighter just exactly where he'd ended up pressing back. We kept on in that position, rocking gently at the point where our bodies met up, and kissing so hard for so long, that by dawn my lips hurt.

It was just after seven when we heard the kids waking up, and we moved apart fast when they came out of the bedroom. Right before Gene started asking what they wanted for breakfast, he leaned over and said, "There's nobody saying we have to do anything at all," and I could tell by his voice that he meant every word. After that, the day passed around us like a slow, fuzzy dream.

Later that afternoon, we were standing side by side at the stove and frying up quartered potatoes for supper when he turned to me and smiled for no apparent reason, looking square into my eyes the whole time. We were standing there side by side frying up potatoes with bacon and onions, with our pasts spreading out behind us. We stood there in what might have been the actual middle of our lives, and trying our best to understand and make peace with our separate histories as they'd come to exist. I imagined us positioned at the midpoints of two elaborate time lines, the sort that are famous for unfolding from the pages of the *National Geographic*, marked and illustrated with minute drawings along the years by events large and small, and that were connected all at once to both nothing and everything between us. And right before I opened my eyes, Gene kissed me where I stood by the stove, saying, "Jeez, who are you, anyway, Sleeping Beauty?"

GENE AND I had grown up together in overlapping alcoholic households. Our occasional twin remembrances were of an unsettling past, and though we rambled through shifting perspectives, the truth ran in a relentless current between us at times. Our parents had been friends in high school and on into college. Both of our fathers played trumpet. All four of our parents sang in choir, bound by youthful, and actual, talent. We'd shared a childhood of musical fathers, who, even when sober, had cried at local productions of the Messiah. Gene had played baritone poorly in the high-school marching band his father directed. I'd inherited my own father's instrument and played trumpet all through high school. I won awards and played solos every year, the same as my father had done, then I gave up music when I entered college. The instrument had been sitting in a dusty corner of my mother's living-room closet for over seventeen years, and even catching sight of its gray leather case still made me shudder.

My father, dark and handsome as a boy, had dated Gene's mother until my mother moved to Michigan from Oklahoma as a high-school sophomore. Gene's mother had a habit of complaining that she'd lost out to my mother's southwestern, twanging-voiced, cowgirl appeal. After his death, my mother once told me that my father'd never loved her the way she'd have preferred being loved: like friends first, and lovers sometimes. At times, however, she confessed she missed my father for another reason, for what they might have shared if they'd only been able to talk.

I WAS nine the year Gene's father and mine took us along to the cabin on a hunting trip. I remember the drive up north to our cabin, both families stuffed in two equally low-riding station wagons, yet I'm not sure why I was included in the actual hunt. Given to fits of crying over dead pets and books with sad endings, I was a pensive and fleshy child, not a logical choice for a hunting companion, and my being drafted for that position filled me with a sense of melancholy. Our fathers drank straight from the bottle—Jack Daniels, Jim Beam, Wild Turkey—but never in front of their wives. Gene had stayed at the cabin that afternoon with our mothers and the other children. They'd hooked up a black-and-white television set and sat around the table eating potato chips and French onion dip and watched a John Wayne movie.

Dressed in a heavy wool jacket, I went with our fathers to flush out game, lumbering ahead of them as they'd ordered, at the edge of the fields. At one point, I lost my sense of direction completely. Half an hour passed before I stumbled out into an open field where both men were standing with their rifles up and pointed directly at my head. My father put down his rifle, then walked across the clearing and lifted his hand in front of me. He removed the leather glove from his left hand and then slapped me twice across my face. "You might have been killed," he said, an odd smile resting on his cold lips. The air in front of his face clouded with his breath, and the smell of whiskey was mixed with the scent of woodsmoke. "Walk the edge of the field," he said then. "Don't come back until I call you. Walk quietly, not like a cow."

It was Gene who finally found me that night, and long past the sun going down. I was sitting in the dark corner of an old shed at the edge of our property. The walls were papered with twenty-year-old issues of the *Saturday Evening Post*, and I remember leaning against a crate of jelly jars, the fruit inside gone mottled years past and black as bad meat.

Gene was ten that year, and came looking for me with a flashlight. "You okay?" he said when he shone the light in the shed and discovered my face. I wanted to explain how I'd never been hunting before, but I felt fat and clumsy, and I couldn't speak a word when he patted my head. He tried to make me feel better by telling me girls had no sense of direction, and I told him that was a dumb thing to say. "I know," he'd shot back in a grin, "I'm a dumb kind of guy," and then he held my hand as we walked back across the fields to the cabin.

My mother'd said, "Well, it's about time," when Gene and I walked back into the cabin. She never noticed the bruise blossoming under my eye. Not that she'd showed.

TWENTY-ONE YEARS later, I'd run into Gene at my father's funeral. Early that morning, a lakefront wind had risen up from the west, driving off a damp September drizzle. The wind blew steadily all day, and by early afternoon, the world seemed surprisingly bright and warm. As I stood beside my mother at the cemetery, the sky turned to a midsummer blue.

Gene was the tallest man at the cemetery. He stood near the back of the crowd at the grave site with his children on either side. We hadn't seen each other for ten years.

"I'm divorced," I told him after the service. The wind blew my hair back from my face and the heels of my black pumps sank into the cushion of grass beneath us. He'd grown a moustache and lost a little hair, but his teeth were still little-boy white and as square-edged as Scrabble pieces.

"I'm divorcing," he answered.

"Same verb, different tenses," I smiled, and when he laughed his mouth pressed two perfect dimples into his cheeks. He'd come back to the town we'd grown up in to go back to school and was working part-time for a local oil company.

"Come by," he said as he climbed in the car where his mother waited for him at the edge of the narrow lane near the burial site. The heads of his children floated like two blond balloons against the back window. "When you're in town," he added, folding his height into the driver's seat.

"You never know," I'd called out. "I just might."

TEN MILES outside of Clare, Gene stopped the car for ice cream, making the fifth time in four days. I've had my braces on my teeth for ten months. I eat a lot of ice cream, which Gene's kids think is great, since they're living on foodstamps and never buy ice cream with their groceries. Gene didn't complain when I pointed out the gas-station-deli-dairy store. "I know," he'd sighed, "two scoops of strawberry cheesecake."

GENE'S PARENTS and mine had gotten drunk together every New Year's Eve, and we remember it well. They drank at our house, and my sister and I went to theirs. My sister and Gene's were the very same age, three years older than me, and they'd both been the same kind of mean.

The New Year's I was thirteen, they locked Gene outside on the icy steps in his plaid flannel bathrobe. They let him back in when he started to cry, then we watched a black-and-white midnight thriller about giant insects. When the hard-put-to-find-a-solution scientists finally dropped a boulder on the enormous spider, Gene said, "Look at that gore." Gore. What a word. I'd been nobody to him. My sister had liked him in a noisy way. She tickled him sometimes until he wet his pants. Once, when I tried to join in, he called me a "zombie witch." I said he was "so mean." Then I shut up. My sister had green eyes and wore violet mascara. She had soft blond hair, and it was thick at her neck. Her teeth were as straight as the edge of an envelope, and she bit her lower lip until it was puffy and pink, all the time watching Gene from the side of her eyes. She'd acted like she owned him, even at her absolute meanest.

IN THE middle of eating my ice cream, I dropped the white plastic spoon at the edge of the gravel driveway. Seven motor homes were lined up for gas, and I stood there outside of the car in their backwash of fumes, looking at the spoon on the ground. Gene said, "Here, hand it to me," and reached over from the driver's seat. He cleaned the spoon with the tail of his shirt and handed it back.

GENE HAS the prettiest mouth I've ever kissed. His moustache falls down on either side thick and soft, and his teeth are so smooth and slick that I almost sigh when I feel them with my tongue. Sometimes I watch him when I know he isn't looking,

looking him over like some great big feast. He likes to play games with the kids and knows all the jokes to turn arguments off. Sometimes when the kids start picking little fights, Gene'll say stuff like "I oughta slap the taste right outta your mouth," or "I oughta kill all of y'all," and they'll start laughing right off every time. He's never laid a hand on any of them around me. He wouldn't even bite my neck, not even a nip, not even when I begged him to.

SO WE took our kids to my family's cabin, where our fathers had holed up drunk. My brothers and Gene used to go up there with them, and Gene had a whole pile of stories about all that. He showed me two bullet holes in the wall of the cabin, right next to the refrigerator. "They were made from the inside, you know," he said, and I stood there for a minute and shook my head. I didn't need to hear the rest of that story.

I'D TRIED to leave my ex-husband on my twenty-fourth birthday, two weeks after Tad was born. I'd just about gotten away, but my ex came home unexpectedly early from army maneuvers, with two pounds of pot inside a paper grocery bag. He'd used half his monthly paycheck to buy it from a guy on post, and intended to sell it right there from our trailer, though I could tell he'd end up using as much or more than he'd sell, as his eyes were already wild.

My ex-husband had two kinds of stoned. One had him eating cereal out of a four-quart mixing bowl with Rice Krispies spilling over the edge, the whole box dumped in with five tablespoons of sugar and a full quart of milk. Other times he went around breaking windows, especially if he couldn't work up the money for a case of cheap beer, saying, "Idiot. Idiot fat-girl," as he checked all my hiding spots for money that he'd known of.

The day I'd meant to leave him, the car was all packed, and I'd traced the route I would take to Michigan across the pages of the Rand McNally. But my ex had grabbed me and pushed be back into the trailer. He'd slammed my head against the headboard when I tried to work free. Then he turned me over, and I breathed the sweaty smell of his face off the pillow as he worked himself inside of me. I bled for two weeks after that, and I cancelled my postnatal visit. Five months later an army doctor had repaired my tears, saying, "Jesus, this time just let yourself heal."

ERICA CLEARLY likes to hang out with me, and our second day up north we took a walk all alone in the woods near the cabin. "My mom says my dad's not my dad, did you know that?" she asked, smiling, but with a little quiver snaking into her voice. Her teeth were too large for her ten-year-old mouth, buckling one over the other, but I could tell she'd grow into them, even if they stayed a little crooked. She told me she'd die if she didn't get braces soon, "just die," and I told her I could remember how that felt.

We had followed the deer run into a sun-dappled clearing, and the grass in the clearing was low to the earth and meadow-like. In the center of the clearing, a double-trunked willow swung its budding mane toward the ground. Three salt blocks rested at the base of the tree, and they were sculpted and rounded where the deer had licked grooves down into their hard white surfaces.

"He's your dad," I said, the truth rocking willy-nilly inside me. I rested my hand on her shoulder as she bent to examine the salt blocks. At the edge of the clearing, the pines rose up and shadowed the needle-thick floor of the woods.

"My dad hates to hunt," she said, staring down at the salt blocks.

"Me too," I answered, then I reached down and took her hand.

OUR SECOND night in the cabin, Gene started feeling we'd gotten caught up in a time warp. The six or seven radio stations we could bring in played nothing but old love songs, day and night. At first it was funny, and we'd chuckle and say, "Jesus." Late at night it became disconcerting, when every song was some bothersome, passion-drunk version of "Love me forever, don't ever leave, me, I'll die if you do, now that I've finally found you." One or both of us would race for the radio, spinning the dial for a baseball game.

I RAN into Gene again two years back at the annual Christmas Eve service in the church where we'd both been baptized as babies. He came up to me in the foyer after the service, pausing briefly in awkward stillness as I put my arms around him. Then he hugged me back, harder than I expected, my face pressed up against his warm chest. I could have stood there forever just breathing him in.

I wrote to him off and on after that, just sending out friendly "Hi, how's life?" kind of banter through the mail once a week, and at first just to do it. He wrote back a few times, even though I'd stated early on that I didn't expect him to write back at all. The first year, writing to Gene had provided nice breaks between teaching and grading papers, but later I'd felt myself changing. At some point past the first year, I was startled to realize I'd begun looking forward to writing each letter, and knowing that had started something odd and roped inside me. Some weeks I ended up writing three different letters, and then tearing up the remaining two after choosing one to mail off. It was usually the shortest.

When I had time the next summer, I drove home to visit my mother, and that's when Gene and I started doing things together. We rode bikes with our kids and ate ham sandwiches at his house. Once he let me ride his trail bike, and I fell and knocked the skin off my knee. He helped me clean out the cut in his kitchen, then told me that I'd be okay. The whole next year I stayed away from him on purpose. My heart beat too crazy when I saw him, and sometimes I had dreams about kissing him.

I stayed clear of him on purpose up until two months back. That's when I'd driven home through the spring rain to show him my new car, the only new car I've ever owned, and a shiny blue reason to see him. That's when I said, "Let's drive out in the country." We'd followed the mile-marked county roads through the night to the oil fields, out to where the wells dipped horse like into the pastures, and where the flames of the towering burn-off valves lit the fields, rising up like giant candles. And somewhere at the end of a dark gravel turn-off, I'd asked if I could touch him. After the first kiss, there was no turning back.

EVERY NIGHT at the cabin, Gene had set my travel alarm for six A.M. We fell asleep so close I could feel the soft hair on his arms, stretched out in front of the fireplace beneath the same blanket. He snored in enormous wide dragging breaths, but I didn't mind. At dawn the alarm worked its way into my sleep as he crawled over me to curl up on the daybed under the window. "The kids," he said. "You know."

"Yeah, yeah," I'd complained, half-asleep and half-mad.

MY MOTHER lives alone in her house in the middle of Michigan, in the house my father had built for her the year they were married. She lives in the house where all but her first child had been conceived, where she'd watched her children grow up. Even though she's been redecorating bit by bit for the past three years, she says she doesn't want to make any big changes. "It's not so much the money," she said last Christmas when my brothers and I offered to replace her kitchen cupboards. "I helped the carpenters mark and set the hinges, I hung half the doors," she explained. "I know my cupboards look beat-up," she laughed, "but I like them that way, they're old friends."

My mother lives in her house full of memories, finding comfort in what remains. She's placed framed photographs of my father on all the dressers and tables, so he can watch over what is left of her life.

GENE'S MOTHER is divorced and lives with her cat just four blocks down from my mother. My mother and Gene's occasionally talk, I would imagine about us, guessing at what it is Gene and I do or don't have going. We are all of us guessing. Our mothers live in that town full of streets and schools and fading pasts. They are stirred by the bustle of the university, threatened by the disrepair of college rentals, and noisily frightened by all the new strip shops on the business route. For our mothers, everything has changed and keeps on changing, and they ask, rolling the sixty-odd-year-old whites of their eyes, if and when things will ever stop.

I have lived many lives since my own childhood there, yet the town seems insistently unchanging to me. There is a bedroom there in a house near campus where I lost my virginity while stoned, and far too young. Sometimes when I visit, I put on my headphones and go jogging, as that is a new-found release, running the streets that I walked to their ends on younger feet. I pass houses in which I played spin the bottle. I put on my headphones and run through the town as the sun flushes the day into night. With the music pumped into my ears, I pretend I am part of a movie. My body complains as I move with my heaviness bouncing against me in defiance. I run past the house where my father grew up. I run past the church where he sang in the choir. This is the town where our mothers live, where I never played sports or went to a dance with a date on my arm. This is the town where I learned how to kiss, and I run through the summer streets, a prodigal, sweat-heavy daughter, racing neck and neck with the past.

THE CAR was full of sand and we were bumper to bumper with weekend vacationers. We'd climbed to the top of the Lake Michigan dunes on a day so bright we'd had to squint just to see. We'd been draining sand from our pockets and shoes all weekend. Now I felt like my heart had begun draining into my hands, that I was dying from the fingertips up.

INTO ALL of this came the analogy. "I'm distant at times, you noticed?" Gene said in the car, twenty-two miles from where we would part. I could've let it drop, but it felt like a dare, as if he were saying, "Notice the distance. Observe it. Pay heed. It is a necessary distance I exhibit." I know that feeling. I grew up crazy. I lived in a madhouse. I was taught not to feel. My father's drinking held us all suspended, and we bludgeoned our hopes, because that was all we could do. No one ever got close enough to challenge how our hearts were bound. And now Gene was lifting a bottled-up hopelessness between us, and I felt myself resist.

"I know you," I said as Gene nosed the car into the passing lane. I waited for him to clear the front end of an eighteen-wheeler, then I went on. "It's like this," I explained. "I think you're kennel shy. That's what happens to dogs when they aren't raised as pets. You've seen them—the stray circling the picnic, the mutt in the alley. They won't look at you. Their ribs show through, and you can even see their hearts beating if you ever get close enough. But they know—however vaguely or uncertainly—that people mean food. But people can also mean a smack with a two-by-four or a bullet between the eyes."

"Kennel shy," Gene said quietly. His eyes moved between the rearview and side mirrors, then he slipped into the right-hand lane. "There we go," he said, dropping the speed back to fifty-five. "Kennel shy," he repeated, then he lit a cigarette and turned down the radio.

So I went on. "They might have an odd, unsettling memory of kindness, of being stroked gently, of falling asleep at the foot of a bed once, somewhere. So they circle closer, because they might get to eat. That's why they keep on circling. That's why they keep their distance," I said. "Like you."

UP NORTH near the dunes, we'd visited a Native American pottery shop, a little square cedar building with big windows in front that faced the lake past the highway. The shelves were filled with replicas of artifacts, along with bowls and vases and mugs. We'd bought an eagle-feathered and clay-beaded ceremonial pipe for the kids, and Gene informed them right off it was only for looks and not for use. I bought a little jade green ceramic urn that was wide at the base and narrow at the neck, made and signed by the resident potter, a slim-hipped Chippewa named Stan. He stood an inch taller than Gene, though a good sixty pounds lighter, wearing clay-spackled Levi's, and with two perfect braids. I studied his thin fingers as he wrapped the urn in two sheets of gray tissue paper. He moved slowly as he worked, explaining that the jar was a replica of those his tribe once used in ancient burial rites. He said his people placed herbs and medicine inside the urn to ward off dark spirits. "Why did people stop doing that?" Erica called from where she stood, looking at the different colors and textures along the row of urns on the shelf.

"Oh," Stan smiled. "First we ran out of burial land, then we ran out of tradition, I guess. Some people are going back to the old ways, which is good." He looked up at me then, fitting the wrapped urn in a small brown bag. "Good thing to remember the past before we forget it," he said. On the glass countertop near the register, there was a small plastic sign reading, "You break, you pay," and Stan noticed how Gene had looked at the sign and then laughed. "We get a lot of people coming through who get careless," he explained, "like this was a flea market kind of joint."

Our last night in bed, I'd fallen against Gene in a tumbling loss of balance, and pinned his arm so hard against the frame of the couch that he'd winced in pain. He groaned then, saying, "You break, you pay," and I kissed his arm where I'd hurt it. I kissed my way up his shoulder to his lips, then I placed his hand flat against my left breast.

"You break, you pay," I whispered back, and he went tight around his mouth and pulled away. "Well," I said, and he placed a cigarette between his lips.

"Well," he challenged, the word emerging to the side of the cigarette. "Well," he echoed, and I'd felt the distance settle in a curtain between us.

"I DO believe I've just been psychoanalyzed," Gene said across the front seat. I smiled, and then I turned away. He was so tall that his head rubbed against the velour ceiling of the car. He's lost most of his hair at the top of his scalp, and I've kissed the sub-bleached down that grows there. I've kissed his ears and his neck and the two perfect dimples I can remember through all those years back to my childhood.

He sat there holding the steering wheel with both hands, and I tucked the tips of my fingers beneath his right hip without looking at him. Even with my hand at his rump, he kept his eyes on the taillights of the car in front of us.

"How much do I owe you for the psychological services?" he said, then followed the curving long exit leading down into the north end of town.

"Nothing," I answered. "Not a red cent."

"That's a bargain," he said as he squinted into the windshield. He fished his Ray•Bans from the front of his shirt, then, with one hand, he fit the bows of the glasses at his ears. "I hear some head docs pull down eighty, even ninety bucks an hour."

The sun hung above the west side of town like a huge copper coin, getting ready to drop away behind a thick-fisted cumulus cloud bank. I sat in the wind-blown silence, aware of the silence itself, then I closed my eyes. The children were sleeping in a knotted pile behind us. There was only a two-mile span left before parting, and it was easier to let it pass in darkness.

With my lids pressed tight, I imagined myself standing at the edge of a jagged bluff, and judging the drop from the edge. If I jumped, I might find myself dead on a shoal bank. But the descent, the insistence of that plummeting draw, was the necessary distance to knowing.

If I jumped, there'd be no time for a midair retraction. If I jumped, I'd fall. Gravity would see to that. In what position or condition I'd land was the only real question, and was the point I was stuck on when I felt Gene's hand brushing gently at my cheek. "You shouldn't worry so much," he whispered. Even though the children were still sound asleep and couldn't have possibly heard him, he whispered as he added, "Let somebody else worry, why don't you."

Gene held his palm against my face for a moment, then he tucked a strand of hair behind my ear. If I jumped, maybe he'd follow—two hundred feet straight down, cutting like a knife blade into the water right behind me.

BLACK BOY IN A
WHITE GIRL'S WORLD

A lean man, narrow and neat, with angular shoulders, James J. Jackson sits at a table in the afternoon lull of the Ramada Inn cocktail lounge. Other than a smooth-faced young boy bussing tables, he's the only black man in the midst of the ice-clinking, quiet conversations of late diners and early drinkers. James watches the boy moving table to table, the slow sweep of the sponge in his hand, the symmetrical positioning of chairs, how he butts them against the tables with a push of his thighs, the tender rosewood nape of his neck where the elastic knot of a hairnet rests. As the boy lights the red, netted-glass globe of the candle at James's table, the match trembles at the wick between his blunt-edged nails. He winces as the flame catches and rides up against the pads of his fingertips, then draws back quickly, flagging the match into smoke as he lowers the candle to the center of the table. The boy lifts one finger to his lips. He pauses, then drops his hand to his side, and James fills with an airless sensation, disjointed and dancing, of not being there at all.

The band plays half their gigs in places like this, in motels off an interstate highway leading into a city. Beaufort, Columbus,

Charleston, military towns, soldiers drinking beer out of uniform, girls up under their arms, girls in short, flouncy skirts the colors of flowers, wandering outside at last call, to kiss next to cars bought on army pay. He's slept in places like this, the musicians taking up four rooms at the end of a hallway, but that's different. With the band, it's like family, coming down at noon for breakfast, waitresses learning their names, everybody staring at them in the daylight as they sit talking, trading sections of the paper, ordering whatever they feel like. With the band he's got history, something to measure and hold on to.

James leans back in his chair, pressing his hand to the wall for balance as he fingers the texture. The walls of the poolside room pimple in sandstone stucco above a fruitwood wainscotting, and he's confused by the overall effect. The stucco and the rounded archways remind him of a Spanish mission that they visited last December outside of Key Largo. Pictures are mounted on every wall, under plexiglass without frames, screwed down like museum pieces. Spotlights run in tracks across the ceiling, trained to the prints on the wall. To his side and behind him stands a white fiberglass replica of the Venus de Milo in the leafy fringed shadows of a potted palm. The jukebox in the back is an ornate old Wurlitzer, in the shape of an enormous chrome-bumpered tombstone. There's one just like it at the 301 burger joint in Tyler, half the records still scratching out sounds from his childhood, back when coloreds had to order take-out, not sit inside eating regular like white people could. But that's where he heard the music, standing at the counter while some teenage boy fried up burgers two for a dollar, then stuck them in a paper sack. He thinks maybe it's the jukebox doing it, the carnival ride colors flashing him back. Or the boy in the white kitchen uniform with his finger to his lips. He's not sure.

At six foot five, he's the tallest man in the bar. Every few minutes he lifts his hand to his face and tenderly fingers the glitter, a diamond stud punched into place through his left nostril. There's a little tug of pain when he twists the post, and he likes how it feels when he rolls it between his fingertips. He's positioned in a burgundy leather captain's chair at a table in the back near the pay phones, facing two gray-suited men. His knees rise two inches above the edge of the table, and he sits a foot back, angling, then dropping down again, slowly, on the tips of his snakeskin Tony Lamas. Every half hour the bartender comes to their table, toting a fresh round of drinks on a cork-lined tray. He comes to their table like clockwork, red cummerbund, red bowtie, looking like the lost member of some wedding party, without so much as a wink or "Come here" from the other two men.

James is wearing his favorite jeans and a starched, pale blue shirt with silver-rimmed pearl buttons. Without a belt, the jeans ride low at his hips, and they're faded down the fly and worn through at one knee. At his collar, a black bolo tie meets in a noose beneath a polished oval of rose quartz. Miss Elvira believes in the spiritual power of crystals, calming, especially quartz. Especially the pink kind. He sits at the table and talks with the men, and sometimes he just listens. When he talks, he leans forward, looking first at one man, then at the other. His hands form a tepee at his chin, and he breathes deeply between certain phrases. Both men lean forward when he speaks, twisting their heads in his direction, ears tilted, cocked to catch the low drifting refrain of his voice. When he listens, he lifts his eyes from the table, making a slow circular sweep of the room. He moves his eyes from the print of a lavender iris on the far wall, lingering over its womanlike folds, dragging his eyes to the door, and then across the room to the window looking out on the pool. Sometimes he sits perfectly still with his lips slightly parted, lifting his hand to his neck. The quartz warms in the tracing of his fingertips. He studies the people who come in and out of the bar, the men and women carrying slim leather brief-cases, calling out to one another, shaking hands, meeting for drinks and business. He has never done business before.

For the recording contract, he will have to rename himself. There are already plenty of Jacksons, the studio tells him. There are too many men named James. He will have to become someone new.

To do this, he's spent two days with the studio's lawyers in the Ramada Inn lounge at the junction of highways leading into Savannah and up into South Carolina across the bridge. The company has booked two rooms for the three of them. James stays in one room alone.

From time to time he goes to the jukebox in the afternoon twilight of the air-conditioned bar and slides a few quarters from his fingers into the machine. He punches in numbers, then waits until the music starts up, winging his hands across the buttons like a keyboard. Seven times in three hours the blue and red lights of the Wurlitzer pulse between "Chain of Fools" and

"A Rainy Night in Georgia." But even with the music going, he can't shake the feeling, tight, like he's stuck in a dream. Last night a blond fleshy woman named Ginny had followed him up to his room after last call. "Is it true what they say about black men?" she whispered as she wiggled her slip down past the pale twin mounds of her hips. The inside of her thighs were soft, pliant and dusty and sweet with talcum.

He ran his tongue against a blue thread of vein that sloped toward her nipple. He could feel her pulse against his lips. "Depends what they're saying," he'd smiled.

Both lawyers insist the nose jewelry is dead-on image-making perfect. "You could even go with a gold hoop," one suggests, and the other nods in agreement, bobbing like he's connected by a string to his partner. But they're struggling with the magic of renaming him. From the time he could walk, James had sung every Sunday at the Tyler Bethel Baptist and Pentacostal Church of Christ. "We need to get rid of the choirboy image," the lawyers urge. "That's the trick. Ditch the halo. Clip his wings."

James has lived among whites all his life. He knows when to talk and when not to. Last week his brother called, asking for a front. "Just a temporary loan," he had said. James told him no, that the money was all on paper at that point.

"You playing the game," his brother complained.

"No, man," James argued. "This is business. A square deal."

"Yeah, you playing white men's games, nigger."

James had his voice to send him to high-school state choir festivals, setting him up alongside the sons and daughters of Tyler's own. He sat next to white girls on the bus rides to musical competitions, girls who wore pink blouses and pastel sweaters soft as rabbits, girls who smelled of gardenia and had peppermint breath, freckles on their cheekbones and leading down their necks. Girls named Amanda, Crystal, Ashleigh, Marybeth, Heather. Sometimes, at parties, he'd ask one of them to dance. But he knew not to ask for a slow song. Not white girls.

Standing in front of his graduating class, he sang a capella in the humid gymnasium, rising on the stage in his midnight blue gown, lifting his arms into wings as he sang. The townspeople went silent in their folding chairs as James opened his young tender throat with "Go forth to life, O child of earth!" His careful tenor sailed up through the fans in the ceiling, the strains of the hymn rinsing over the crowd like a bath.

James had been raised by his mama's parents, Miss Elvira and Black Bob, and was told that his voice was a gift come down from God. He was a quiet child, and his voice had allowed him to move through the world, allowed him to be asked to stay for supper at the brick houses of his white-boy companions, houses with inside plumbing, with carpet to muffle footsteps, doors with screens. His grandparents raised him up after his mama moved to Alabama with a soldier, saying someday she'd come back for him. She never did. His family had always been poor, living for five generations in the silver wood and tarpaper shanties back of Kicklighter's funeral parlor. Miss Elvira had been born in the house James was raised in, and she took in ironing like her mama had done before her. "Getting by," that's what she called the work she took in. That's what she called heating the seven-pound iron on the stove, nursing her blistered fingers, rubbing linament into her ankles after supper. She also doctored poor folks, neighbors and river people, delivering babies and mixing up salves and herbs for what ailed them, including broken hearts. Most people paid what they could for her medicine, a couple dollars, live chickens, or eggs, and some paid nothing at all. Mending hearts was free. Black Bob made a few dollars here and there doing odd jobs when his bones didn't hurt. He'd had a real job once, working for the county road commission, but one day he'd fallen under a backhoe, and his legs had been crushed. After that, he'd never had any steady type of work, not that James could remember.

James had lived poor all his life, but that day, when he sang in the high-school gymnasium at seventeen, he felt some power rising up strange and new within him. E. Henry Broadwell, the captain of Tyler High's football team, out of which an occasional black player made all-state, never to be heard from again after winning a full-ride scholarship to some small Southern college, took it upon himself to invite James to his graduation party under the bridge at the river on Prison Road. That night, some-where around midnight, James found himself deep between the trembling thighs of a young white girl named Clarissa, whose father ran the auto parts store west of town, and from that moment on, his gift became newly articulated. Those were the places a voice like his got you, and he liked that feeling, liked how his gift got girls wet and willing and roping their arms at his neck.

James earned a four-year scholarship to Savannah State, and

he made it through with a liberal arts degree. After he graduated, he went home to Tyler every fourth weekend to sing in the choir, walking uptown on Saturdays with a blue pin-striped button-down tucked in his jeans, just like the white boys from town. At night he'd lie on his back in the bed by the stove in Miss Elvira's kitchen in the space where he'd slept as a child, staring at the moon through the window. On Sundays he'd wake to the chill of the room, moving barefoot across the cool linoleum to light the stove. He'd dress quietly in the kitchen, then fry up eggs and three kinds of meat—sausage, bacon, and ham—until Black Bob wandered out in his union suit, crying, "Well, well, just look how the Lord has blessed us." The other weekends he smoked hash and drank wine with the seven people he shared a house with near campus in the city, and sang with the house band at the Tenderloin Ballroom.

Working the Tenderloin made James a local notable, and he sang with a band called Ripple and Ice, three black guitarists from State with a lesbian singer named Sasha, born black to a white mother, with breasts so full James couldn't help but want to put his lips to them and nurse her into loving men like she did women. They didn't have a regular drummer to speak of, though occasionally one of the men from the music department of the college sat in, and that's when the band really shook. They played blues, old Motown, smoky ballads their mamas had sung, James's tenor raking through the lyrics, then rising up in a howl, holding off on one line, hanging on to another. Every so often some pale, slow-moving girl would sidle against him between breaks, passing him notes on napkins and matchbooks.

Sometimes they'd follow him home. They'd run their hands the length of his body, studying the color of his skin. "Don't worry, it doesn't rub off," he told them. Some of them acted like they wished that it did, saying, "What's it like being black?"

Eventually, the band became a kind of legend, attracting local musicians to come into the Tenderloin and sit in beneath the mirrored ceiling and heartbeat of colored lights. And the band made good business for Willie B. Lamb, the proprieter, who up until James came onto the scene, had been forced to rely on mud wrestling and male exotic dancers to draw a crowd. The clientele had shifted some with the band, but money was money to Willie B., and he found he liked the odd lot the band drew, even the gay boys and lesbians coming in to see Sasha sing. At the end of each set he'd bring Sasha a spritzer with a little pink umbrella poking out between the ice, and they'd sit at the table during break making jokes, Willie B. hunkered over and watching her face the whole time.

One afternoon, James and Sasha had come in early to fix a short in one of the amps, and Willie'd hollered to where they stood in the back of the bar. "Girl, you're so skinny I can hear the wind whistling clean through your ribs," he called out. Sasha dropped her eyes and smiled, then shook her head slowly left to right as she soldered two wires in place. "In fact," Willie added, "the two of you put together don't but barely make one whole person."

"Is that so?" James asked, winking as he met Sasha's eyes.

"That's just about so," Willie B. answered. "And I'm going to stand here and fry you up something good to eat," he added, slapping two frozen patties of beef on the grill. Five minutes later he shouted, "James, get on up here," and James made his way to the front of the bar. "Now, mind you," Willie B. said, pushing two baskets of burgers and fries across the bar, "I genuinely like the girl," he said, low and whispering as if making an apology. James met his eyes then, and he added, "But I can't bring myself to think of nothing but a woman beneath a man as natural sex."

"What you mean, 'natural sex'?" James had laughed, and Willie B. went red down to his collar, and got busy washing glasses behind the counter. "She looks pretty natural to me," James said then, jerking his head in Sasha's direction. "Damn natural," he chuckled.

"I mean natural the way God intended it to be," Willie B. stated tersely as he dipped and rinsed the glasses.

"I see," James teased gently as he picked up the baskets of food.

"Go on, now," Willie B. ordered impatiently, acting mad, but even so, James could tell Willie B. lay awake nights thinking of Sasha's breasts, same as he did.

The summer after James finished at State, Sasha laid a tape on him, saying, "Here's some shit might work for us." She'd spent two years at Eastman, and her sense of chord structure was good. Up until then she'd held the band's vocals together, sliding against James's lead in a haunt of descant, coming into work with sheets that she charted herself. But that tape was like nothing James had ever heard, and he felt the old power lifting up within him so certain he couldn't sleep. She'd made the tape in Los Angeles with two singers she'd met back in New York who were under contract to a West Coast studio. Alone, any one of the three voices might have gotten a rise out of someone, but tracked together, overlapping and threading in dense harmony, their voices were like something he'd heard in a dream. Some of the lyrics were in French, some in Portuguese, exotic and tracked in layers of pidgin between the running harmonics, not mattering what they meant.

James was so certain about what he'd heard on the tape, that Sasha helped him work a deal with Willie B. for tickets, and the two women from the West Coast had flown into Savannah for a stint at the Tenderloin, and their agent followed out two weeks later. On a hot August evening, they put on a show for him, and the next morning James signed a tentative contract.

That's how he finds himself drinking vodka gimlets with two white lawyers in the Ramada Inn lounge, attempting to invent a new name for himself on a yellow legal pad between the three of them. Late in the afternoon of the second day, after repeated trips to the hotel bathroom to facilitate the creative process with what Rolland and Emory, the two by then trembling and flinching lawyers, call a "necessary indulgence," they've moved from the inventions of "Triple J" to "2 Jay Jackson," both names having a bad-boy rapper's appeal, an angry kind of attitude the three of them would like to avoid. Somewhere near five o'clock, Emory moves from "Two Jay" to "Toujaise Jackson" on the legal pad. Rolland sits shivering and deliciously cocaine spastic. He's got white eggs of saliva in the corners of his mouth. "Cut the last name, and we've got it," he grins. "Toujaise," he coos, dramatically pursing his lips. "It looks French, sounds French, and it's liquid, lush. Who gives a flying fuck if it is French?" and it sticks.

James becomes Toujaise that summer, and he grows his hair long and winds it into dreadlocks, ragged coils bobbing against his neck. James becomes Toujaise for the studio contract, working the Tenderloin, sticking drugs up his nose after last call, hammering out lyrics at the typewriter on a desk in his room at the top of the house. Sometimes he finds himself running a line up the sweep of a thin white girl's nose, some vaguely and temporarily interesting wisp of girl with pink nipples, ushering her out the door of his room before morning, her legs still wet from his sex.

HIS STARDOM surprises him spitless at times, especially now that the studio's told him they'll be touring with a top-name band come December. Especially like now, when he's high, when he's done a few lines of good blow while cranking out lyrics with Sasha and the boys in the band. Toujaise smokes steadily in the dark studio at the back of the building off Oglethorpe Square. He could work out of a studio in Los Angeles, but he doesn't know Los Angeles. He can make deals in Savannah, feel his way around, work the turf, know who's for real and who's not. He's happy living in the house where he started out, even if his housemates still call him James and go into fits about his clothes.

The singers are working their voices through the synthesizer, picking up on a beat the drummer laid down just before squirreling chalk up his nose. Now the drummer—who has just this minute changed his name to Manda Lashra, though Sasha says it sounds more Hindi than Nigerian—is sitting cross-legged on the floor in front of the speaker columns at the front of the room. The room is carpeted with blue and gray and yellow wool up to the ceiling baffles, and the walls fold in and out every three feet for sound.

The studio belongs to Vinnie Falsetta, and was originally used to make tapes of polka and zydeco bands. Every so often Toujaise puts in those musicians as they pass through the studio. He picks them up for a set or two, sixty-year-old, white-haired polka kings with dentured smiles squeezing an accordian line over Dog Leg Danny's keyboards, an occasional Haitian steel drum or finger piano running next to Sasha's cool alto, all coming off like only Toujaise knows how to make it happen.

Vinnie's happy having them work out of his place and even put in new electrical wiring after the first month of blowing circuits right and left. Vinnie's got money, but nobody asks how he gets it, though Toujaise's helped him unload bales from his trawler at night, the name of the boat changing weekly. Vinnie's thin and tall, and his hair is steel at his temples. He tries to slip Sasha a C-note every week or so, but she's not playing his game. He's got one front tooth set in gold, a little border of precious metal framing the white of his tooth, and nobody messes around with him, or so he says. And he's standing back in the sound booth, smiling when the newly named Manda Lashra lifts a thin ebony recorder to his beard, parts his lips, and then plays over the drum bed on tape in an echo of the lyrics in his head.

They're all sweating blood on this last cut for the album, sweating blood and blow and Wild Turkey through their pores. Sasha's purple tee hangs in a shadow between her breasts, sliding wet against the angle of her skin. Vinnie's cut the air on, but they've heated up the room again with sound and breathing. There are seventeen musicians on payroll, and they are mostly related in some way, if not by family then by history. Toujaise lifted the half-dozen male back-up singers straight from the Baptist church choir in Tyler. One is his brother, born to his mother in Alabama and shipped back to her parents twenty years ago, when she'd had to do time for bad checks. One is a brother born to a river girl, light-skinned and fathered by Toujaise's own daddy, the same year he'd been born in Tyler. He was ten when he'd found out about him, following Miss Elvira down to the landing to doctor his croup in the middle of a winter night. He'd stood at the end of the cot in the shack, staring into a dusty, green-eyed version of himself. Three of them are distant cousins, but they are all part of the Toujaise brotherhood, that's what they call it, though Sasha takes great pains to deliver sermons on the oppression of women, and how if she didn't love them all first as people, she'd be just as happy to cut off their male-dominating organs.

Toujaise is calling the album *Black Boy in a White Girl's World*, and the studio's approved his title. The agent asked him to explain it, since it wasn't the title of a cut, and James had gone quiet in the studio. Sasha stood behind him, saying, "Spill, let's hear it."

"It's this 'thang,'" he said, and he'd had to breathe deep to get it right. "It's this thang in my head that won't let go."

Sasha just laughed, saying, "It's some kind of thang, nigger, like that thang hanging there below your belt." But the rest of the band just shook their heads, going on about the title, saying, "Bad. That's bona fide bad."

Sometimes when he gets all the shit out of his system, Toujaise tells Sasha he feels like a rip-off. "No, baby," she says. "You for real." He's starting singing with a stilt to his voice, and the weed puts a scratch on his lyrics. When he's clean he takes off the Toujaise clothes—the black top hat, the wire-rimmed blue glasses that aren't even prescription, the short madras caftan, the black spandex tights—and he wears button-front jeans and a leather jacket, stuffing his braids up under a little red wool cap. But even that looks good on him, even that is no disguise for his new persona, and the girls who hang around the front door of the building follow him to the back lot where he parks his jacked-up El Camino, a car he bought from a white high-school boy in Tyler. Sometimes he lets one, even two girls in the car, and they ride around town taking turns with their heads in his lap, knowing just how to make it last with their perfect pink tongues. And he feels like he's living out some kind of demented dream half the time, and bent out of shape because he's liking it.

The first stanza is looping through the speakers, and it's Toujaise's voice alone at first, going,

> What I say is IDENTITY,
> number one, not number three.
> We've worked too hard,
> and worked for free,
> diggin' in the white man's garden.

The band hangs with him, hangs with this thing about whites, and they nod back and forth, heads rolling with the sound as he works it into the music.

Sasha got into it with him one afternoon in the studio, saying, "Then how is it you only go poking your thang into white girls? Explain that." The band had gone silent then, dropping back against the walls and watching as the two of them faced off beneath the microphones.

Toujaise stood there a moment, then took off his glasses and winced. He rubbed circles at his temples with his fingertips, then he lifted his eyes to Sasha's face. "Power," he stated. "It's this power thang."

Sasha crossed her arms at her waist. "So, now the band's going good, it gives you power over the white man? You think you being a little bit famous give you the power to take whitie's woman? That ain't a black power thang, boy, it's what men been doing to women all along." She dropped her head, shaking it side to side. "Power," she snorted.

"Not my power," he said, then he sighed. "Theirs." Sasha lifted her head and shrugged in confusion, her face tight and defensive. "Theirs," he repeated.

Sasha stood with her hands on her hips, then spread her lips in a sudden flash of smile. Toujaise nodded. "And you just a nigger-boy plaything for them?"

"That's about it," he laughed, and Sasha just kept on smiling.

The back-up singers are tight in a bunch at the far end of the studio in front of the glass of the sound booth as Toujaise's voice loops through the studio again.

What I say is stealin' time,
bust my ass to make a dime.

I've got children dyin' of hunger,
working so hard and not gettin' any younger, get gone . . .

and then his voice breaks off in a wail of sliding lament that they
tape a capella, and the singers pick up on it in the studio, every
single one of them closing their eyes at the microphones,
picking up on Toujaise's lead.

The three women, who have until this moment been listening
with their heads lowered, lift up their solemn eyes and put their
voices down in matched intervals, and it's all so perfect Toujaise
waters up behind his glasses. The two women from California
are permanent with the band now, and they've been doing this
kind of work for seven years. Aubrey and Tanika are large-
hipped, myopic twins with heavy breasts and wide feet. Sasha
is slender and mixed. She's Tanika's lover and nobody cares,
because everyone is a part of this scene. Aubrey's got a degree
from Berkeley and she plays keyboards. Sasha never graduated
from Eastman, but she's good and can translate into French.
Tanika cooks when they travel. The three of them are tight as
cheap shoes, that's how they talk about themselves.

Melvin, the small black man in the sound booth, is staring
through the glass as he stands at the mixing boards. His fingers
work the keys north and south, getting it all down with his eyes
on Toujaise. He can cut out the stray noise and coughing when
he mixes the master. He's been working studios for seventeen
years, and this is a once-only sound.

Toujaise is sitting on a table in the back of the studio. He's got his head down and the ear-set to his cheek. Then he stands and walks two steps to where his own mike hangs from the ceiling.

If his eyes are open, the blue glasses hide them. He points to Dog Leg Danny at the synthesizer keyboard, and Danny cuts to the original instrumental bed, a steady four-four drum stroke and progression of piano chords. Toujaise rolls a pencil between his palms at his waist as he starts to sing. The tips of his fingers are quivering.

> And God, this river is as dark as my beating heart,
> and I don't know why.

That's a good line, and he repeats it.

> Daddy always gave us love forever,
> but I just can't find that door.

Then he pulls in a thick breath and leans into a rasping prayer.

> I would save my own life, if I only knew how,
> I would save my own life if I could.
> I would hang on the cross,
> if I thought it would save us,
> if I thought it would do any good.

Then he smiles and repeats the last fragment.

Melvin stares through the glass of the sound booth. His fingers float like dragonflies over the mixing-board. He keeps his eyes on Toujaise's face as he drops everything down into silence, and nobody says a word.

THE KID'S
BEEN CALLED
NIGGER BEFORE

Toby sits in the back of the green Pinto wagon and sings until the windows fog up. He's got a dozen fresh batteries, four brand-new tapes, and the music's pumping loud through the headphones. Over the vibrating thrum of the engine, he tilts back his head and belts out a favorite line. A few more words, then he closes his eyes, the melody floating loose in his throat. Then he goes quiet, stroking his red hairpick in a steady four-four.

Marty lifts his eyes to the rearview mirror, then he smiles and shifts into third. Colleen is still filing her nails in silence beside him. She stops for a moment when Marty puts his hand to her knee, shakes her dark bangs from her eyes, then starts up with the file on her other hand. Marty looks from the mirror to her face. Toby picks up on a song behind them, following along in open-throated abandon. The car quivers for a moment in the pull of the storm front, and the wheels skate off toward the shoulder. Marty looks from the mirror to the road to Colleen, taking his hand from her knee, then he looks to the road again. "That kid has got one set of lungs," he smiles.

Colleen sticks the file in the glove box, smacks it shut, then looks back at Toby. He's snapping his fingers and humming between his lips, low in his throat for the bass line, then switching to the melody in a whine through his nose. Toby's father is black, but her looks have come through in his cheekbones and the crossed overlap of his two front teeth. In the dwindling sunlight, his eyes are shot through with shards of green, and his hair is a net of tangled curls. "Like his father," she says to Marty, settling back in the seat and facing the windshield again.

"I guess," Marty replies, squinting into the oncoming traffic as he exits the interstate and merges with the two-lane highway. "But you're musical," he says. He remembers the first time she came into play at the Four Corners bar where he drank every Saturday night. He'd been sitting at a table near the small red half-moon of carpeted stage, splitting pitchers of Stroh's with the boys from the bakery. They were waiting for Jonny "Love 'em and Leave 'em" Longnecker to walk out with his midnight blue electrical guitar and stand there in front of the shadows of his brother and his drumset. Jonny was local, twice divorced, drove a 1965 mint-condition red Mustang with a black leather top, and did the books for his family's excavating business. His brother, David "Davey Jay" Junior, was five years younger, and state-certified in heavy equipment. Weekdays, the Longnecker brothers worked out of their green aluminum-sided garage west of town on Industrial Drive. Weekends, they made music at Four Corners and had a way of getting both lucky and in trouble with women.

That evening, when the manager announced Jonny was down sick with the flu, the crowd had booed and hissed, lobbing peanut shells and wadded-up cocktail napkins at the stage.

They were still making noise when Colleen walked out and adjusted the mike, planting her feet on the stage as her fingers trembled against the stand. She sat curled around her guitar on a stool for a moment, waiting for the crowd to settle down. "This is a song about someone who used to love me," she said softly, without even introducing herself, then she'd leaned forward and started to sing. By the end of her very first number, even the die-hard Jonny Longnecker fans had settled into listening, including the boys playing pool for serious money in the back. When she finished, they pounded their cues on the floor until she started up again.

She'd played three sets that night, and each song was a story of something she'd lived through. Just after midnight, one of the boys playing pool took off his Stetson, dropped a handful of quarters inside, then passed it to a nearby table. The hat made the rounds of the bar, and by one it was filled with dollar bills.

Nobody in the crowd knew much about Colleen, except that she worked the counter at some party store and wasn't local, but she was pulling stories from their lives as she sang about hers. Marty sat there that night, studying how her hair had a way of falling forward, hiding half her face and making shadows across the top of her guitar. Every so often, though, she'd lift up her head for a moment, wincing as she lingered over certain phrases, then dropping back down again. That's what he remembers as he turns on the headlights, saying, "And you're the one raising him, after all. He's your kid, too."

At home in the white clapboard rental house, it's just the three of them going through their lives together, and most of the time Colleen forgets Toby's half-black. Then she's reminded, quickly, uncomfortably, at school carnivals and potlucks, or in lines at the IGA. People startle, turn away, then twist back in a slow double-take. They look from her face to his and don't even pretend not to gawk. Toby says he's used to it. He shakes it off, saying, "Never mind, what do they know?" When people nearby get to whispering and staring, Colleen moves in close to her son and smiles like nothing is wrong. She puts her hand to his shoulder, though she knows she can't really protect him. Most people drop away once she's there close beside him with her smile in place, though every so often there are some who smile back and forth between their faces in a curious sort of compassion. "Your son has such beautiful eyes," they say brightly, or, "My, he's a tall one, all right."

She'd met his father over thirteen years back, a lifetime ago, she tells Marty when they talk. Larry played drums, working as a studio musician when Motown was still in Detroit, and he sang in a sweet liquid tenor.

She'd been working at a record store in the city for ten months, moving from Saginaw to live in a flat with her sister, Patti, and helping out with the rent. Her parents had made her move, saying it was the least she could do, seeing as she wasn't working a real job. Playing guitar in a band at the bowling alley didn't count as regular employment, they'd informed her, and neither did holing up in her room all day writing lyrics in a notebook and practicing chords. On her twentieth birthday, her father came home from his job at the cement factory and handed her a Trailways ticket for Detroit. Two days later, he'd driven her downtown in his truck, loading her guitars and two suitcases onto the bus, the same as he'd done with Patti.

Her sister studied art at Wayne State, and modeled nude in the evenings for figure-drawing classes. That money was off the books, collected in an old coffee tin during class, and Patti laughed as she counted the money at night, spilling it out on her bedspread. "Wouldn't Daddy have a fit if he knew about this?" she giggled, but Colleen said she wasn't so sure he'd even care.

Neither one of them had a car or more than a few dollars left after rent, even with the modeling money, but Patti got food stamps and managed to keep them fed. Patti had a skinny, red-haired boyfriend in the army, Terri Hawkins. They'd been high-school sweethearts, and he'd given her a blue star sapphire ring the night before he reported for basic. Ten months later, he got killed in Vietnam, somewhere near the delta and eleven days short of coming home. Patti and Colleen had stood on the asphalt at Detroit Metro, in a cold, icy rain the week before Christmas, not quite believing that the gray military casket coming down from the belly of the plane was really Terri. Six soldiers in dress greens stood at attention on either side of the coffin, and Patti waited there without moving or speaking as an officer saluted her, handing over an American flag and a small plastic bag of Terri's personal belongings.

The two of them sat up that night in their apartment, and drank a gallon of pink chablis as they sorted through his things at the kitchen table. Other than his dog tags, there wasn't much to look over, just a day book and photographs, pictures of the men in his unit—dirty and anxious-faced boys hamming it up in the jungle sun, boys in government issue T-shirts and fatigue pants staring into the camera, the last people to see Terri alive. Patti put the pictures in her jewelry box, along with a letter that had never been finished, her name and Terri's looped together at the top of page one in a circle of penciled hearts. "Dearest Patti Cakes," it began. "Sarge sent the papers to the chaplain. If we meet at Fort Bragg, they can get us married in a week." The next morning they smoked a joint to take the edge off their headaches and followed the hearse along the interstate to Saginaw.

The army had sealed the casket, saying that's how they handled those things. Mrs. Hawkins had thrown a fit at the funeral home, insisting she be allowed to view the remains of her oldest son, arguing that no one would ever know if that was really her Terri in there. The Methodist minister followed her into the bright lights of the room in the funeral home basement. Later he'd stood with his arm around her shoulders as she greeted people in the parlor during visitation, white-faced over what she had seen. Patti told Colleen that she didn't need to see anything more than what she'd found in the bag of his belongings.

They went back to their apartment after Christmas, and Patti hung her ring in the middle of Terri's dog tags around her neck. After that she stayed stoned and quit eating. Sometimes she'd sit at the kitchen table with the metal tags pressed between her lips as she studied her art books and sorted seeds from a bag of dope. Colleen wrote a song about that. She'd never had anyone to write about before. Except herself.

She'd met Larry two weeks after the funeral, coming into the record store during a January blizzard. He wore a black leather jacket and a black wool beret. He spent two hours bent over the record bins, holding albums up to his face and reading the credits on the jackets, then he came up to Colleen at the counter. "You cut me a deal on these records, I'll take you to dinner."

She studied the length of his fingers as he drummed on the glass countertop. "I don't cut deals for anyone," she stated. Then she looked up at him. His eyes seemed to fill half his face. They were perfectly round and his lashes were as long as a girl's.

"Well," he smiled, "then just dinner."

The next day Patti said, "Don't go bringing that nigger around here."

"Black," Colleen said. "The word is 'black.'"

"The word's 'nigger' in my house," she corrected, fingering the silver tags that hung against her heart. "And how come he didn't get sent half the world away to die?"

One week later, the two of them found a place of their own, and Larry stayed home and wrote songs while she worked in the record store. He even wrote a song for her once, banging it out on the old piano they'd traded her twelve-string guitar for, working on the melody in their apartment off Inkster and Eight Mile. She hadn't liked the lines he put in about the color of her eyes, but she never let him know, since he'd starting insisting she was unnaturally suspicious. Those days she showed up at the studio, he said he could just feel the heat rising up between her and his girls singing backup. Then she got pregnant, and every few nights he stayed out until dawn. And then Toby was born, and he stopped coming home at all.

In the car now, she tosses her head side to side, fingering the
pulse at her temples. She'd thought she'd forgotten all that. The
car shimmies in the wind, and she looks over at Marty, at his tall
slender body, and her heart starts winding back down. The first
time he kissed her he'd put his hands to her face, then pulled
back her hair from her eyes. He's got silky blond hair, baby-fine
and hanging forward over his high, freckled forehead. The
heater's not working right, and he's zipped up his navy blue
parka to his chin.

"Hi, stranger," he says. "Where you been?"

"Thinking," she says. "But I'm back."

Marty likes old songs, songs he knows the words to, but he
tells her he can listen to just about anything. He bought her a
stereo and says he's ignorant about music in general, telling her
he doesn't mind listening to love songs by black men, if that's
what she likes. Those are the songs she plays when she gets into
one of her moods, songs sung by men who can't let go, give up,
figure out, deny, or withhold all the loving they're feeling for
someone. Or some other somebody else.

Toby rewinds a tape in the backseat, punching buttons, mut-
tering, "Nope, nope," then hissing out "Yes," and he starts to
hum. He likes it when his mother sings. He likes how she puts
songs on the stereo when Marty leaves for work, watching
through the living-room window as he backs out the drive. She
stands at the window, singing every word perfect as Marty heads
down the road into town for the night shift at Wonder Bread,
her hips swaying under her nightgown and an arm at her waist.
She holds a hand to her shoulder and turns and swirls across

the carpet, slow-dancing all alone, not the way she has to move with Marty, who says his feet are too dumb to dance and makes them all laugh.

Toby clears the fog from the window on his left and looks west to the tree line. They're thirty-two miles from their home in the middle of Michigan. His father sent him a Walkman UPS from Los Angeles for Christmas. He called Christmas evening and asked Toby to come out to visit, saying "You grown now, boy. Ought to let your old man have a look-see." But his mother said L.A. was no place for a twelve-year-old kid. Toby wants to go just to know what it's like, to meet the musicians his father works with, not to stay, he told his mother. To visit. He looks back at the trees where the sun is setting, wide currents of red running through the dark bank of clouds. The wind brushes sheets of snow over the stubbled fields, and he breaks into singing again.

"You okay?" Marty asks, reaching over to touch Colleen's cheek, and she nods, pulling at the threads of a button hanging loose on the front of her coat. "Look at the sunset," he says, and she turns to the window beside him.

Marty stars at her then, her face taking on pink in the light rising up from the horizon. Then he turns back to the road, drawing away from the center line. "Hey, listen," he says. "Don't worry about that stuff with Dad. He's worked his whole life for Oldsmobile. That's where he gets that stuff about Toby. He's old. And he's mean when he drinks. I'm still glad we went. After all, how long we been together? A year now? And I'm glad that he met you, and Toby took it well, at least as well as he could. He's a good kid, you know."

"I should have let your old man have it," Colleen says low and quick. "I should have given him a piece of my mind." Then she pauses, tightening her eyes in a squint. She'd put off meeting Marty's family as long as possible. He'd been asking for months, saying they could just drive down to Lansing, meet the old man, meet his family, get it over with. She had known it would go like this. "No," she says slowly, drawing the word out. "I should have punched him in the nose."

At eleven that morning, Marty's mother had met them at the door of the square, pink-brick house with green trim. She'd come out on the porch when they pulled in the yard, her lips lifting high above her dentures. She'd hugged Marty and Colleen, then pulled back uncertainly as Toby extended his hand. Colleen held her breath for a moment, then broke loose with a smile as Marty's mother grabbed his hand and pulled him close. "You like turkey, young man?" she asked, and Toby grinned at the ground, nodding as she patted his head.

Once inside the door, Marty's mother got busy hanging up their coats, talking and laughing at nothing as they walked down the short narrow hallway to the living room. Marty's father sat watching television on a sofa by the window that faced the front yard. He looked up only once as they entered the room, then stood and walked past them without saying a word. Colleen stepped back through the doorway, watching as he pulled on a heavy wool coat in the kitchen at the end of the hall. Then he pulled on his gloves and went out to his woodpile in the back of the house, splitting logs until the meal was laid out on the table.

Rhonda, Marty's sister, wheeled into the yard around noon in an old blue Impala. The back seat was hopping with her kids, an eight-year-old-girl with brown pigtails sticking out above her ears, a ten-year-old boy with a broken tooth, and a baby in a yellow snowsuit that she pulled free from the car and bounced up on her hip. They came busting into the house, loud and cold and hungry, Rhonda wobbling on high heels, swaying with the weight of the baby, her skinny bare legs pimpled with cold down past her knee-length leather coat, rolling her red-rimmed eyes. "Darryl's too hungover to make it," she said, holding a cigarette between the tops of her red nails. She took off her coat in the living room, saying, "Men, we'd be better off without them most the time." She held her cigarette in one hand, and then held out the other to Colleen. "And I'm Rhonda," she said, "seeing as nobody around here knows enough to introduce us," then her voice trailed off as she followed her kids to the kitchen, asking "What's Daddy doing chopping wood out there in this kind of weather anyway?"

Marty's mother set up a little television in the kitchen so the children could watch the New Year's parades. Toby played on the floor with Rhonda's baby girl, making a game out of rolling a blue rubber ball into an empty Cheerios box. Colleen peeled potatoes and yams with the women and listened to the sound of the ax splitting logs in the yard.

Toby turns off the tape and slips off the headphones, then looks out the window again. It's dusk and it's started to snow. Large star-shaped flakes float sleepily through the twilight. He writes his name on the window, then adds "Nigger" beside it, and pulls up his hands in the sleeves of his coat. He studies the back of Marty's head, the headlights of the oncoming cars catching the loose hair at Marty's shoulder in a white glow. In the future, he imagines Marty might look like the man he met today, old, grizzled, a hearing-aid plugged into each furry ear. Toby's grown used to Marty, to the odd, nervous way he drives, how he teases him about girls now, and he likes how he's sweet on his mother. When Marty stood up at the table and shouted at his own father, "You son of a bitch," Toby'd gone all cold inside.

"Marty," Toby said as they loaded themselves back in the car. "Don't worry about the kid. The kid's been called nigger before."

"That doesn't make it right," Marty answered, turning the key in the ignition and fluttering the gas pedal as the engine squealed and caught. "Does it?" he said, so loud and mad that Toby just sat there in silence.

From the moment they started dinner, Marty's father had sat at the table and studied Toby, staring first at him, then staring at his mother. He'd stop to take a bite of food from his plate, then start looking back and forth again, chewing slowly and breathing hard through his nose. Halfway through the meal, Colleen put her fork down, then folded her hands in her lap. "Excuse me," she said to Marty's father. "Would you mind explaining why you need to keep staring at me and my son?" The old man sat there slicing turkey on his plate for a good full minute, then he lifted up his face.

"Lady," he said then. "You got a nigger for a son," and everyone stopped eating.

Toby'd been called nigger before, but when the old man spit out that word, he couldn't do a thing except sit there and stare at his plate. His mother sat in the chair beside him for a moment, then she'd stood and put her hand on his shoulder. Marty rose from the table a second later, yelling at his father, then the three of them put on their coats. Colleen had gone pale, begging a cigarette off Rhonda before they walked out to the car, even though she'd quit smoking two years back.

The heater fan's busted, and Marty flexes the ache of his fingers against the wheel. When they get to the house he'll build a fire in the woodstove and play video games with Toby. He bought the Nintendo for Christmas, for all of them, he'd said, saying he'd always wanted one, but really, he wanted it for the kid. Colleen had been complaining about Toby going downtown to the arcade, spending up his quarters in the game machines. She worried that someone would get him, someone who hung out in places like that, looking for boys.

Colleen wraps her coat around her, turns up the collar, then says, "I really wouldn't have punched your old man." His father had frightened her, and that made her mad. She doesn't like being scared. She's worried that Marty will look at her differently now, that he won't like Toby so much anymore, and that someday he'll start feeling like he's in too deep, that he'll get an itch and take off. "I'm used to being alone," she says.

Toby leans forward between the two bucket seats, the headphones circling his neck. "I'm sorry I ruined the day."

"What do you mean, 'being alone'?" Marty asks.

"You didn't ruin the day," Colleen says to her son. "I mean

how it was before you," she tells Marty. "When I lived all alone for ten years with my kid. That's what I mean."

"I like how it is now," Toby says, his voice rising in a tremble. "I'm sorry I spoiled the day," he adds, sinking back in the seat.

"You DIDN'T spoil the day!" Marty yells. "And I like it too. I like how it is. Nothing is spoiled or ruined. Is it?" he says. "Is it?" he repeats, taking a left at the Seven-Eleven.

"Just don't you turn out like your father," Colleen warns, and she feels her voice shaking and holds her purse tight in her lap. "Don't you ever call my kid nigger," she says, and she lets it out, her tears running hot down her cheeks.

Toby looks down the road in front of them. The snow is falling in heavy wet flakes in the headlights, slurring beneath the tires. "Nigger," he says quietly. Colleen lifts her head, shaking it in disbelief.

"Nigger," Toby repeats loudly. "Coon, spear-chucker, jungle-bunny, Rastus, ape-face, shithead nigger, asshole nigger, lazy nigger, dirty little nigger." Marty looks back over his shoulder, the car lurching once to the right, and the tires grate the shoulder. Toby leans forward, placing his head between theirs, taunting "Nigger—Nigger—Nigger" in a schoolyard singsong.

"Toby," Colleen scolds in a whisper.

Toby gives a whoop and leans back in the seat. "That's all, folks," he says. Marty starts to smile, and he looks at Colleen. She'd holding her fingers to her lips. Then she leans sideways and falls against him, lifting her hands from her face.

The wiper blades move slowly with the weight of the snow,

cutting two perfect arches against the glass. Colleen drops her head on Marty's shoulder, and he ropes his arm around her neck to pull her close. Her hair bobs below his chin as she laughs, her voice rising up in a thin loose music he can barely hear.

MISTRESS OF CATS

Lydia called me ten days before Christmas, saying, "Louise, Daddy's dying. You need to go home." She'd flown home from Dallas at Thanksgiving, with Amanda, her lover, and had been quick to inform me that just being in Tyler had brought it all back.

"Thank God he's too weak to beat Mother," she sighed through the phone. "I can't go back there again," she half-laughed, a note of hysteria threading crazily through her voice. "It's your turn, though believe me even as I'm speaking, I know what I'm asking." Then she paused for a moment, and I could hear her drawing up her breath before going on. "After all," she stated firmly, "he ruined both of us on men. I can't love them, and you can't keep them."

"I CHOOSE not to keep them," I reminded her curtly, and not for the first time in our lives.

"If that's how you still want to see things," she acquiesced briefly, then added, growing distracted and angry, "if you truly see things at all."

"Lydia, don't," I sighed then, the knot of my jaw rising up against the receiver. "Why do you keep on doing this to me?"

"You would've kept Tommy Ray," she challenged right back. She's always been quick on the draw.

"Don't say that," I answered. "Just let's please leave that be."

"You know, he's still there in Tyler," she sang out, her thin soprano racing two-noted along the wire from Texas to Georgia. "I saw him," she added, her voice drifting curiously and soft as she spoke. "Louise, you can look at this world any which way you choose, but there's one thing I know for certain," she said.

"And what's that?" I inquired, feeling wary and not quite sure of just what she was leading up to.

"When Daddy broke your heart over Tommy Ray, he broke it for good," she answered, and then quietly hung up.

"CLOSE YOUR eyes," Tommy'd said.

"All right, already, they're closed." I was poised on the edge of Daddy's white-painted Grumby, rocking forward and with my back to the plum of the dropping sun. Tommy bounced down the steps of the porch to his black pick-up in front of the house, and then the door opened and closed with the buckle of the damaged panel where we'd slid into a pine on our way to the river to swim naked. "I'm waiting," I stated, holding the flat undersides of my fingers against my eyes.

"Quiet, or you'll wake your daddy," he warned as he took the steps slowly, then I felt him standing in front of me again. "Open your eyes," he whispered, in that same gentle tease of words he used when we undressed together in the dusty daylight of his parents' Sunday-quiet bedroom.

"Open your eyes," he'd whisper, while his parents were off

praying in the church on the outskirts of Tyler, their heads bent solemnly as they sat in the dark pews of the First Baptist chapel, most probably beseeching God for our very salvation. "Open your eyes," he'd whisper as he lifted the chenille-tufted coverlet, folding it back with the weight of the bedding. He'd be standing there shyly proud and naked, and me lying under the cool sheet with my eyes squeezed tight, wishing us into darkness.

"Open your eyes," he whispered on the porch, urgent and secretive, tapping the toe of his workboot to the tip of my white summer pump. I opened my eyes to the sterling silver buckle I'd bought him last Christmas, a heavy silver oval embossed with the Confederate flag, and centered at the waist of his dun garees. Ever since Christmas, he'd been wearing the buckle on the tan leather belt that I'd tooled for him during tenth-grade shop class. I'd designed the belt myself just special for Tommy, with two long alligators meeting face-to-face at the buckle, and his initials stamped along the back of the space between their tails. The belt was cinched at his hips, and right above his middle he was holding an orange kitten in his hard-knuckled hands.

The kitten was so small it fit inside his hands, with only its head poking up and the long fluff of its coat flowering out from between his fingers. I sat there for a second, not quite believing what I saw, and smiling at how its tail was hanging down in a sleepy vine from between his wrists. "Tommy!" I whispered.

"Happy Sweet Sixteen," he smiled. "It's what you wanted," he said then, his teeth showing even and white between his anxious lips. "Isn't it?"

"It's perfect," I answered reaching up for the kitten, and it came into my hands without a sound, without a question or curiosity, limp and warm and full-bellied lazy.

"What'll Daddy say?" I whispered.

"He can't say nothing," Tommy answered flatly. "It's a gift. Can't go giving back a gift," he said, placing the top of his finger to the white silk throat in my lap. "Nothing wrong with a little gift," he'd said, his voice dropping off low as he turned away and pretended to be looking at something on his truck.

IT HAD taken me three days to get everything in order at Coastal Federal before driving home to Tyler, since I'd been completing the paperwork for half a dozen loans at that point. Vivian Armeni, the loan department supervisor, had approved my leave of absence the minute the form hit her desk. In my ten years with the bank, I'd accrued eighty-seven personal days, not including the seventeen weeks of paid vacation time I'd never used up. Even though Vivian assured me I could leave right away, she wasn't surprised I stayed late for three nights and insisted on tying things up. She'd promoted me herself to work as her assistant and had stood firm in requesting that I be given my very own office.

"That's the thing about you, Louise," Vivian stated, coming into my office and saying goodbye the night before I left. "You can sit there and work like nothing else matters. The world could be on fire all around you, and you'd still keep going until everything was perfect."

"Well," I smiled, double-checking the last pile of papers on my desk for signatures and dates, "I can't tolerate leaving business half-done."

"I'll call you at your mother's if I have any questions," she said, then she stood up and paused in the doorway for a moment. "This bank will miss you if you ever leave us," she said gently, then she stared into my eyes without speaking.

"Now, why would you go to talking like that?" I asked. "I'm only going off for a couple of weeks, then it's back to work. Just like always," I added, though even as I said it, I felt curiously sad for some reason.

Vivian and I had known each other since I'd hired in as a window teller, and I'd been her assistant for more than two years and was making seven times over what I'd started out at. Both of us knew that most girls never worked their way up past the counter like I had, especially without a college degree. "I don't know," she said then, right before turning to leave. "It's just this feeling I have."

"You and your feelings," I called out as she left, though I'd been unsettled as soon as she'd said that. Through the years we'd developed a professional friendship, and nine times out of ten, her feelings had a way of being right.

I drove home from Savannah on a bright, cool day the week before Christmas. The sky had thinned out blue overhead, with clouds piling up in cumulus banks in the rearview mirror behind me, near the coast. The last half of the trip was forty miles directly inland on the two-lane military highway. That road's always been a peculiar stretch of nothing, one mile the same as the next and the one before. The pines and scrub brush split away at each side, and the army's clay-dust heavy-vehicle trails run parallel to the highway the whole length.

The forestry division was burning off overgrowth that time of year, and fingers of dark, damp smoke curled up from the weeds to the edge of the asphalt. Just past the turn leading into the back gates of the post, I met up with a string of army jeeps and canvas-backed trucks heading south to play war games along the gulf at Walton Beach, their tires dropping clots of red earth along the road. The camouflaged faces of the soldiers peered down from the trucks. The men squatted at the tailgates of the personnel carriers, the smoke from the cigarettes whipped from their lips by the wind, their white smiles a surprise in the mottled shadows of face paint. They looked straight into my eyes as I swung out to pass them, their hands flat to the bills of their caps, rising in a mock salute, an invitation, and meaning nothing whatsoever to me.

"OPEN YOUR eyes," Tommy'd said at the edge of the pond. "Open your eyes."

Tommy's father was sitting in a flat-bottomed boat in the very center of the algae-fringed water. "I was thinking we ought to bury him here," I suggested, wiping my hands at my eyes. The kitten lay wrapped in a pale yellow towel at my feet. I'd left the house without shoes, and the grass beneath the trees was cool and damp at my toes.

"I don't think he suffered," Tommy said, his voice so gentle I almost swelled up in tears again.

"He's dead now," I said. "It doesn't matter."

"You go on, now, and sit there in the truck. Daddy's got a spade behind the seat. I'll make a good spot for him."

The kitten lay in the towel, and only his head showed, like some pretend baby doll wrapped up for play. "He was just little," I said, then Tommy's father gave a shout out on the pond as his line shot down taut beneath the green glass mirror of the water.

"You go on now," Tommy said, and he followed me back to the truck, his hand at my elbow. I turned up the radio, spinning the dial from station to station, covering the sound of the spade going into the wormy earth. After a while, Tommy came back to the truck, his fingers muddy and damp. "It isn't right, Louise," he sighed, dropping the spade into place behind the seat. "A person can't just go doing something like that. It isn't right the things he does."

"You going to stop him?" I said then, and not caring one bit how angry I'd sounded. "You going to stop him, Tommy Ray? Tell me that."

I LET up on the gas as I passed by Brandell's onion fields, the migrant Haitians and local blacks bent at the waist, ankle deep in the pungent soil. They stood chopping weeds between rows, their heads dropped and covered, some in bright kerchiefs knotted at the forehead, and others in straw skimmers and old cast-off felt hats. Just past the fields, two small, white crosses were standing at the base of the telephone pole next to the village limits sign, marking the spot where Lydia'd said Joe and Paula Broadwell died last July Fourth, high and drunk, with her head in his lap going eighty. On into town, signs rose up at each side of the road, local-made, hand-lettered signs for PECANS, PAPAYA JUICE, VIDALIA ONIONS—THE ORIGINAL. The quarter mile in from the first yellow blinker to RED'S GAS AND PARTY TO GO rolled under the wheels of my apple-red hatchback like a movie I'd seen in some old false-fronted theater too long ago to remember the name of.

The business district hadn't changed in the ten years I'd been gone, the square, red-brick buildings with their intricate cornices, the striped awnings and unblinking windows—the same, and rising up from the cracked, weathered sidewalks running east to west where the highway name changed to Main Street. The barber shop pole still wound its red and blue illusion across from McDermot's Feed Store, the blue-and-white clapboard filling station had retained the same black attendant, his ashen hands polishing the chrome pumps, a lawn chair unfolded in the shadows under the thick oak to the west of the building. The NO CREDIT sign remained nailed to the tree at eye level, which all blacks knew was meant for them alone, as other folks into Tyler had held standing accounts there for years.

A block past the filling station, I turned left onto 301 at the stop light, and where Kicklighter's Funeral Parlor was still sitting where it had sat for more than eighty years. Lydia'd written me a few years back that Willis Kicklighter had finally gone and converted their upstairs apartment into additional viewing rooms, and moved his family into a house west of town. Growing up, both of us girls had felt sorry for the Kicklighter kids living there in that house, as it seemed a horrifying thought how their daddy's undertaking business went on right below them. Even with Willis's family moving out, the building looked the same, gray-shingled front to back, and the white shutters nailed down across each window.

I drove south past the light, down the 301 Business Route, south past the Tyler farmers' market and livestock yard, past the auction grounds and tall wire fences, south and up over the rise where the drive to the house I was born in spit gravel across the tar. I pulled in the long, narrow drive and rode slowly to the circle of dirt that roped around back of the farmhouse. The house was the same, standing tall and white in the center of the thinly grassed scalp of the yard. Behind the windows, Mother's starched muslin curtains hung in even folds, closed against the daylight and remembered.

Daddy's rocker was sitting out front, just where it always had, held in an expectant backward tilt by the weight of its heavy ladder-back, ghostly and motionless at the west end of the porch.

Mother's black sedan was pulled to the edge of the side porch, and appeared in good shape, though its tires had worn smooth. The car was the only true sign of life.

"THERE NOW," Tommy'd said. "There now, open your eyes." In the quiet of his bedroom in his parents' house he ran his cool palm against the swell of flesh at my hips. "It's okay now, don't worry. The first time is always the worst."

I stared at the white, sloping ceiling, following down to the window across from his bed, looking out on the pasture to the back of the house. "Don't fuss so," I said. "You didn't hurt me."

The sound of my voice in his room of insect collections and 4-H awards seemed to come out of nowhere, unfamiliar and unowned.

"I'd thought you'd bleed," he whispered, sounding worried and turning just then so he lay on his side next to me. He went to running the cool wash of his hands down my belly, then past my belly to my middle, sliding his narrow-boned hand between my legs. He leaned gently against me, his other hand working up my ribs to the rise of by breast, then he lifted his face to mine. The May breeze pushed the border of the ivory curtains above the windowsill, over and over, and slowly, so the fabric went to waltzing back and forth against the screen. "Maybe that's just for some," he said with his eyes on my face. "Don't take it so hard, Louise. Come on now," he said. I could feel his fingers inside me, and the press of his body still wet beneath his belly.

"I couldn't fight him off," I said then, the lead of my voice dropping between our faces. "It was like some horrible dream, the kind where you're scared half to death but you can't even move." I turned just an inch, just enough so our eyes met, so close that his lashes brushed up at my cheek. "Same as he did to Lydia, only she ran off when she couldn't take it any more. She wasn't but sixteen, and she just packed and left. If Mama ever found out, it'd kill her, just as sure as that. It would. She'd die."

"Your daddy?" Tommy asked in a whisper. "Are you saying your daddy?" he said, then went silent as I nodded, holding his fingers inside me so still I stopped breathing a minute.

"Maybe I shouldn't have told you," I said softly, and he'd

answered without speaking, rolling his head back and forth against my shoulder. "It's just that I keep thinking how we promised from the start not to hold secrets between us. Remember?" I asked, and he nodded as he turned away.

When I'd first started wearing his ring four years back, we'd promised to be honest about everything between us, no matter how large or how small. I'd been his first and only girlfriend, and a whole lot of folks were surprised that we'd ended up staying together. Tommy had a head of blond hair that went nearly white in the summer and was so handsome and tall early on, he could've had his pick of any girl in Tyler, even some a grade or two ahead of us. When he first started taking me to school dances, I'd never done any actual dating, and I was curious about him being interested me in particular. While I wasn't shy in general, I was something of a loner all through school, and not the sort of girl I imagined he'd like. Then somewhere in the middle of our third or fourth date, he'd explained on his own what I hadn't been able to figure out. "I don't know," he'd said as we stood dancing slow in the school gymnasium, "but you're the only girl I've ever been able to talk to."

"Tommy Ray," I teased back, "that's not true. I've seen you talking to all sorts of girls." I stayed quiet for a minute before adding, "And most girls are half-crazy over you."

He'd laughed when he heard that, and pulled me close, saying, "But you're the only one who listens when I talk, not that half-hearing that girls take to doing, wondering if their hair's right or who's noticing what. Now, remember," he'd pretended to scold. "I'm an only child, and I got spoiled up good by my mama, as she still believes it's her God-given duty to go hanging onto every word coming out of mouth."

Four years of loving me for listening, and then he'd had to hear my secret. "Jesus, Mary, and Joseph," he'd said as we lay side by side. "Jesus, Mary, and Joseph," and then he went quiet, pulling his hand from my wetness, his damp and bloodless fingers coming up to my face, my scent against my own lips. His tears met my face in a sting of dampness between our cheeks. He lay there with his arms at my shoulders, and crying without making a sound. Inside I was nothing but air.

THE MOMENT my eyes fell on my father's face, I knew that he didn't have long. Mother ushered me through the parlor, her hand at the small of my back, nervous, light, and uncertain. We passed from the quiet, bright parlor into the dark of their bedroom, and she stood behind me, chattering, working her hands at the waist of her apron, then up at her temples, fingering the steely gray spit curls. Daddy took one long look at me, then he lifted up on one arm in the bed, his other arm flagging out from his shoulder, wild and spastic and feeble. "Get that cow out of my house," he cried, his voice thin and whistling with his illness. There was no flesh left between his skin and his bones, only reminders of knotted and angry muscles and the cable of withering tendons.

"Now, Daddy," Mother said, "Daddy, look here at Louise. She's lost weight now, and look how she's dressed so pretty, and all for coming to take care of you. Daddy, tell her you're glad she's here. She's got a leave from the bank to come tend to you. Daddy, it's been so long, now. It's your Louise. It's your baby."

"I know a whore when I see one," he coughed, choking up beads of phlegm, then he spat into a cup on the nightstand. "Get her out of my house. I can't abide a slut in this house."

I stood in the warm, dark bedroom and breathed in the air of his sickness. I stood in the room I'd been conceived in and stared into the blue water of his eyes, his pupils wild and large with morphine. "I'm here to help my mother," I stated. I kept my eyes on his face, and he finally fell back in the bed and faced the rose-garden wallpaper. "You've no say in the matter," I informed him. "No say at all."

Each morning I woke before Mother, stirring surprised in the bed I'd known when I lived in that house as a child. I'd rise early to the sound of semi-trucks as they surged past our drive, pushing into the final stretch before Florida, to the sound of the glossy, loud crows in the spires of the pines out back of the house, to the vibrating chatter of small-bodied birds in the bushes beneath my window. I'd make breakfast while still in my robe, wearing nothing underneath, the breath of the house passing cool between my skin and the fabric as I stood solidly at the linoleum-covered counter, the pattern of gray and red and black and yellow squares faded and bubbled with age. Mother had found fresh mocha java beans at the Red and White, and my pleasure at her purchase of two pounds of my favorite coffee reflected off her face in almost painfully unfamiliar delight. That moment passed between us too quickly, and never repeated itself.

I ate breakfast each morning in my father's chair at the kitchen table, slowly, indulgently, even as he began calling for assistance, and then I would bathe in the old porcelain tub upstairs while Mother began the rituals of caring for her dying husband. After dressing, I helped her unwrap the gauze at his ankles, rubbing cortisone cream into the maps of ulcers that patterned the length of his body. Even with the morphine going through him, he kicked at my hands when I touched him, swearing that I hurt him, that I watered his liquor, his head propped up on the saliva-stained pillows. He kept ranting as I worked beside my mother, his cheeks spidered purple, his eyes rolling, slow and golden with jaundice, as he followed my movements.

He sucked on his gin till the end. Mother nursed the liquor in through his dark, swollen lips, tilting the spoon against the cracked and bleeding split of his mouth, even when he could no longer eat for vomiting. The work wore her out, made her thin, made her cry. I'd hear her at night as she emptied his urine bag, water running in the downstairs commode, the low, gentle sound of her words rising up through the floorboards, the grating of the small rocker as she pulled it up close to the bed. One evening I'd found her crying in the kitchen, and in a fit of vexation, I said she should just let him die. I'd put my arm to her shoulder as to comfort her then, but she'd pushed it away, saying, "Well, you must not know how it is to spend your whole life with one man, and never loving anybody else."

"You're right," I'd said then, facing her back as she wiped her eyes dry with an ivory hankie. "I don't know what that's like." Standing there watching her struggle with the meaning of that kind of sadness, it was clear she wouldn't last long without him.

Daddy died New Year's Day as Mother was bathing him, and at first I wasn't sure that she knew he was gone. I'd come into the room with fresh towels, and his face had been turned toward the door, his eyes open and fixed on nothing. Even seeing him dead, I couldn't help Mother with what needed doing, as I couldn't bring myself to touch him. I stood at the side of the bed, gently resting my hand on Mother's shoulder as she bathed him that final time. She moved in peculiar calm as she sat at the edge of the bed, working the rag against the yellowed bar of soap in the metal washbasin. Even standing close beside her like that, I felt a curious distance between us as she lifted him forward in her arms, so thin he seemed made out of nothing. I moved back as she pulled the gown from his shoulders, watching as she washed his sagging chest, his flaccid white belly, the winged bones of his hips, and how she pulled the adhesive tape from the catheter. His genitals lay small and nestled between his powerless legs, a shrunken souvenir.

At last she folded his arms at his chest, then ran her finger the width of his wedding band, then up to his blind eyes, pulling the lids gently down. And then in the quiet morning, we stood, one at each side of the four-posted bed, and we lifted the sheet to his chest. I had thought we would cover his face, but Mother paused briefly, hesitant, her tongue at her lips. "Daddy," she said. "Daddy, may death be a happier place."

I stayed on for a few days after the funeral then had to go back to my job at the bank in the city. The morning I left, Mother promised to come see me in June. "Won't that be nice," she had said, patting my hand as I sat in my car. She stood at the front of the house as I drove off, lifting her arm once in a small, gentle arc of goodbye. Early that spring, when the ground soaked up rain, Lydia called in the middle of the night and told me Mother's heart had given out.

I went home to Tyler to tie up the estate, and I slept with the lawyer, a dark, smiling man I remembered from the high-school debate team. He lifted my breasts to his lips as we lay in my bed upstairs at the back of the house. He said, "Why don't I remember you from school, Louise? I'd remember a girl like you." I told him I'd been different back then, and that fifteen years was an awfully long time, time enough to forget someone like me. Then I told him to remember me now as I kissed my way past his navel, and he trembled against my lips. He said that he would. By all means.

I hired a man out of Reidsville to come auction the things I chose not to keep. I did not want the vinyl recliners, the colonial sofa, the dishes, the drapes, or the tractors and tools in the barn. After the sale the auctioneer stood in the quiet, dark house and said, "Louise, with just the antiques here it's really quite nice." I smiled and took off my coat then unbuttoned his shirt, running my hands through his curly blond hair to the back of his tender neck. It was my house now.

I'd never intended to come back to Tyler to stay. When I'd left, I had said I would never come back, but that's what all fat girls say when they race to the city fresh out of vocational school to snatch up a job in an office or bank. That's what all girls say when they pile their hair on top of their heads, then look in their mirror and see their mothers staring back. That's what girls say when their fathers have ruined them and beat them, and the closest they've ever felt freedom is letting some gentle, tall, pimpled boy work his fingers down into their pants.

I kept telling myself I'd go back to the coast in a week, maybe two. But the lawyer called up every morning, driving out after lunch, and the rain kept coming down, night after night, beating steady at the roof of the house as I slept, exhausted from our afternoon bed play. The storms finally dropped off into drizzle and mist, then after two weeks I woke up to sunlight, the sky stretched tight and wide and blue all the way to the horizon. The lilacs swelled open in Easter purples, wagging on branches under the windows, and the farmers came out and pulled their shirts from their shoulders as they struggled in the fields. They turned their pale, naked backs to the sun as they dragged plows behind their tractors, tilling and turning the damp soil, and I stayed. I said, Let them keep their city apartments. Let them keep living, asshole to elbow.

So, I lived in the house with two heavy Blue Persians named Asia and Africa, who still had their balls. My men friends said, "Lou, you should get those cats fixed. That's why they keep running off, don't you see?" I pushed a cool hand down the front of their pants and said, "Maybe someone should do that to you." The cats wandered off, but they always came back. Done in. Hungry. Wanting canned salmon.

When Mother was living she had always kept dogs, collies and shepherds with dark grapes of ticks at their necks, dogs whose piss burned the edges of bushes and dried in streaks on the trees, the stink rising up after rain. I took the last one off to be shot when Mother died, and paid twenty dollars to have it done. The owner of the filling station knew someone who'd do it, but still he'd insisted on asking, "Ma'am, are you sure?"

In May I took a job uptown at Danner's Department Store, and the women I worked with said, "Don't you get bothered out there at that farmhouse, all by your lonesome and all?" I said, "No, I have cats." And I had my men friends, but I didn't tell them that, didn't tell them how many or why I could smile all day, how sometimes it was all I could think of while lining up testers of perfume on the glass countertop or trying a lipstick on a customer's wrist.

Most all my men friends didn't like my cats, and they complained they left hair on their clothes, said they'd leave fleas in the bed. I told them I kept my cats clean. They said, "Look how they lick themselves," as the cats curled forward at the foot of the bed, spreading their legs and nosing between their furry hindquarters. When my men said they'd like me to do that to them, I did.

I worked in cosmetics at Danner's, a position I valued but didn't need. I could've lived years on the money that Daddy had left behind, squirreled and invested and holed away, kept from us all by sheer meanness. But the job gave my life order and it helped me meet men. They came into Danner's to shop for their wives, for their girlfriends and mothers, and I knew just the ones I could catch. They came to my counter looking for something to patch up a fight, something just right for a birthday, some little expensive sweet something or other. They never knew what they wanted, and I showed them Giorgio bath gel,

Opium dusting talc, Chanel No. 5, and glittering body mousse —"for that special occasion." When they asked in confusion what scent I preferred, I lifted the hair at the nape of my neck, bending just so across the glass counter, my eyes to the mirror one aisle over in accessories, and I told them, "Smell." With their breath at my skin, I lifted my eyes from the mirror to the pale planet of their faces. "Obsession," I whispered.

LYDIA AND Amanda drove out in August to pick up some things in their van. I'd promised them a pie safe, six pressed-back chairs, and the cradle we'd both used as babies two lifetimes ago. Lydia laughed right out loud one afternoon after lunch when I explained in great detail how I juggled my men friends. Amanda smiled and said perhaps they could borrow a man for a night or two, seeing as I had enough to pleasure myself, and then some. "We're thinking of starting a family," she said as she stood and washed dishes at the sink in the kitchen. Lydia stood to her left drying plates, and she put her hand on Amanda's wrist, tilted her head, then Amanda said, "Oh, go on, you can tell her. You're sisters. Sisters can talk about these things."

Lydia turned and looked over to where I sat at the kitchen table, sorting out the pages of coupons from the Sunday edition, cutting along the dotted lines with Mother's best scissors. Lydia had been with Amanda for seven years, ever since they met back in college. I'd known they were lovers the first weekend I went to visit at their apartment in Statesboro, back of the student union. Lydia hadn't needed to tell me. But she'd wanted to tell me, and she'd cried when she'd said, "We're together, you know," like nothing else ever in her life before had meant so much. And I'd hugged her to me then, just like we'd hugged in our bed those dark nights, trying somehow to save ourselves.

She looked at me there from the sink, tall and red-haired like me, but with her hair cut short on the right, tumbling long down her left cheek, with Daddy's thin mean body caught inside her, padded with breasts and hips. "First, tell me one thing," she insisted as our eyes met. "Aren't there any bachelors left in Tyler?" she asked.

"I'm not interested in getting married," I laughed. "If that's what you're asking."

"Well, not necessarily marriage," she stated, wrinkling up her nose as she spoke. "Maybe something a little more secure, that's what I meant,"

"Do I look insecure?" I teased back, trying to make light of her concern.

"No, Louise," she smiled gently. "I didn't mean it that way. It's just that even with these guys coming around right on schedule, you're still virtually alone."

"Oh," I said then, and turned back to my coupons. "So, maybe I'm alone," I continued, "but at least the rules are clear."

"Right," she answered. "No commitments, no broken hearts," she sighed, then she turned to Amanda beside her. Amanda was short and dark, with a heavy bosom and plump, child-like legs. "Well, Amanda here has been having fits that her biological clock is running out," Lydia smiled, running her fingers through Amanda's thick tangle of hair. "And I'd like a family," she added as she piled the plates in the cupboard. "I'd like to have something that lasts," she said softly, placing her palms flat against the counter with her back to me.

The day that they'd left to drive back to Dallas, Lydia had gotten out of the van for one final hug. "Hey," she whispered in my ear, "don't cut yourself short with these men." Once they had left, the house rose up empty around me. I fretted through the silent rooms all morning, pulling the sheets from the beds, running a wash, filling up time. At noon I decided to make up some chowder and I drove into town to the IGA. Shopping is something I like, wheeling along the aisles like a regular somebody, thinking thoughts about food and my men and sometimes thinking on nothing. I was standing at the produce counters, with the crushed ice wedged in between the celery stalks and broccoli, when I looked up and saw Tommy Ray.

He was standing at the end of the aisle, next to a display of cereal boxes. Debbie, his wife, had her back to me, bent down and talking to two little blond boys, saying, "We've got two boxes at home you haven't finished yet." Tommy was still thin and blond and baby-faced, standing with his eyes on my face, and he never looked away. It's funny how Debbie looked up just then, funny how she looked quick to Tommy, then me, and then back to the boys.

I held both hands on the red plastic bar of the grocery cart, moving through the six feet between us like I was making some commercial for television, smiling so perfect my heart could stop. "Well, hey," Tommy smiled, moving two steps to meet me.

"I'd heard you were back." Debbie smiled as my cart nosed against theirs, her lips lifting up brightly and too quickly, a hand laid to each boy's head as she moved closer to Tommy.

"I guess everybody still makes it their business to know everybody's business in Tyler," I smiled, my face going all hot in a flush of blood.

"Now, don't you look pretty, Louise," Debbie said, tossing her hair nervously around her thin face. She wore tiny cross earrings and a thin silver wedding band. "You have certainly become a citified woman. Savannah must've treated you right. Don't she look nice now, Tommy?" she spoke fast and sweet. Tommy pressed his lips together, smiling wordlessly nodding.

"Thank you," I said. "Your boys are so handsome. They look just like their daddy," I added.

"You going back to the city, Louise?" Tommy asked, just regular and even, like my heart wasn't due to fly out of my chest and land right there in their cart.

"There's no telling," I answered, then he smiled at me and I smiled at Debbie, and I turned and pushed my cart back through produce, leaving it off at the bakery at the front of the store. I sat in the car in the parking lot, turning the air on my face, swallowing down something that felt like tears, thinking just once how Tommy'd cried out my name with his lips wet against my face.

"OPEN YOUR eyes," Tommy'd said. "We've got to talk about this. Lying there with your eyes all screwed shut won't help."

Tommy lay half on top of me still, our legs damp and warm

with sex. "Let's just go off somewhere," I cried. "Let's just get out of this place and go somewhere no one knows us," I begged.

"People get married at seventeen," he said. "We don't have to feel so scared, you know. It's not like we don't love one another. I love you. Doesn't that count?"

"Outside his bedroom window the winter rain had iced the trees in the backyard. "We got till June to finish school."

"We could go nights to those special classes," he countered. "I could go to full-time at Wadell's."

"Where we going to live?" I sighed.

"Here," he answered firmly, just like I should've known.

Then I laughed. "Tommy Ray, you mean living here with your parents, sleeping as man and wife right over their heads?"

"I guess," he grinned.

"You're a spoiled only child, you know that, don't you?" I said. "And what will your parents say?" I asked, and he lifted his chest above me in a shrug. "It don't matter what they say," I stated. "We'll be dead, anyway. My daddy's going to kill us both." Tommy's face went slack next to mine. "That's the truth," I sighed, and Tommy held me tight against him.

SEPTEMBER WAS unusual hot that year, and the weather was distracting, making me restless and unable to figure out why. Work kept me only half-occupied, so I decided to start on the house. I called in a crew to plaster the ceilings and scrape off Mother's old wallpaper and paint the rooms white. I had gray worsted carpet installed from the front of the house to the back, and I set a black leather sectional sofa alongside the parlor windows.

Then, on my thirty-fifth birthday, in November, I met Jacob, a roofer from Statesboro, and for the first time since Tommy I let myself go when he touched me. I knew what I wanted when he came inside me, and I narrowed my boyfriends to three.

Jacob also owned land and rented out properties, and that's how he told his wife he was spending his time when he came out to get me at night. We'd drive out of town with the wind whistling in through the windows, speeding down the coast to Brunswick, or over the bridge to Hilton Head. He drove a Lincoln with dark, tinted windows, windows you couldn't see into, a car full of gum wrappers, hair brushes, baby seats in the back, remnants of life with his family. He ran his hand up my thigh as we sang to the radio, talking about where we should eat, if we should eat, and should we eat in or get takeout. He loved Chinese, so I loved Chinese too, and we'd eat in the car out of white waxy cartons.

Sometimes we went to Savannah and parked down on the river front, then we walked till our feet hurt, finding bushes and alleys and places to kiss on Oglethorpe Square, and he'd say, "I'm young again, Louise-baby, young." Sometimes we never made it out of his car and did it right there in the seat just like some kind of teenage dream, looking out at the boats passing in and out of the river's mouth.

Jacob's last name was Talarino, and I called him my Italian Stallion. One night I straddled his hips and moved real slow to the song on the radio, rocking him close in my arms. He said I sure knew how to move. I said, "Give me a baby, Jacob, do it," and he swelled up inside me so hard that he moaned, holding so tight he left marks on my hips. When I showed him the bruises, he said I was just like a peach, and he pressed his lips to each blue blossom he'd left on my skin.

Craig liked my cats, but he wouldn't admit to it, calling them "Stupid somethings," tossing them pieces of shrimp as we sat eating naked in bed at dusk. Later, we sat on the porch, and I'd brush their hair in the moonlight, saying, "See, aren't they pretty?" and he called me his Mistress of Cats. He was young, twenty-two, and had his own trawler, shrimping the coast and coming inland to see me the nights his wife did their books. He'd arrive smelling of sea-salt and fish-guts and kissing me into silence. Early in December the breeze blew in warm from the coast and he took me fishing under the bridge on Prison Road. I took off my clothes and swam naked where the river ran clear and strong over the sandy bottom and smooth stones. He talked to me from the riverbank, telling me Burt Reynolds had made a movie and filmed part of it right there, did I know that? Then he told me that they should make a movie of me standing like I was, waist deep in the water, as he unzipped his jeans. He said he was too young for someone as wise as me. I walked up the grassy incline to where he stood, then he said nothing at all as I pressed my wet body against him. I took his hands and showed him what to do. He came like a flash inside me. "Not too young for what I need," I told him.

Later that week Eddy Jo drove out right after church on a Sunday. He was peevish and mad at his wife for letting her mother move in with them, putting her up in the bedroom right next to theirs. He brought me a fig tree from his flower shop to put in the kitchen, one I had hinted would grow like a weed by the bay window he'd paid to have put in. The cats sniffed around the soil in the pot and bit gently at the leaves on the lowest branches. Eddy Jo lifted my robe to my waist, his hands to my hips, and I leaned back against him, saying his name, right there in the kitchen as I filled the teakettle at the sink. Then I whispered, "I want you inside me," and we dropped like that to the floor, touching the whole way down, the cats purring and winding between us. In the bright morning light on the small braided rug, I felt him burst loose inside me.

Halfway to February I knew I was pregnant. I had been pregnant before. But this time there was no father to whip my back into bleeding behind the shed, no old drunk to bust my jaw with the back of his hand or to pay off a doctor to pare out the knot that Tommy had tied in my womb.

TOMMY'D SAID, "Baby, what's he done to you? Baby, Jesus, what's he done?" Daddy blew out the windows of Tommy's truck with the shotgun he kept by his bed, and after a while Tommy signed up and went off to Fort Benning.

JACOB PAID for me to see a doctor in Reidsville, a man that he rented an office to. He was a young Jewish doctor from Chattanooga, who said all his life he had dreamed of practicing in a small town, family doctoring, like it used to be. He was blond and blushed easily, but he never once asked was I married, only talked to me about my age. He weighed me every other week and prescribed vitamins, saying thirty-five wasn't old at all, and that

I only looked about twenty-five or six at that. He'd asked my first visit if the baby was planned as I lay there with my feet in the stirrups, and I laughed right out loud. "Completely," I told him.

He'd smiled and nodded, saying "That's nice to hear, then."

Craig took me shopping on Valentine's Day, saying it was the least he could do. We drove to the mall in Savannah, and he smiled watchful and kind as I modeled jumpers and tops that fanned out at my hips. On the way back to Tyler we drove past the trailer park where he lived with his wife. He pointed out their trailer to me, and said, "Don't you ever get jealous about her?" He laughed short and fast when I shook my head. He put a cigarette in his mouth and said, "I do."

Eddy Jo asked first if he was the father. I told him flat out I didn't know, and then asked if it mattered. "No, I don't suppose so," he sighed as the winter wind swept past the trembling dark window, and then he rolled away from me in the bed.

"You listen here," I said, taking his hand, and I placed it palm down on my stomach. "This is my baby. Mine. You can share if you like, but if you get ugly, it's over."

"What are they like?" he asked, rolling back toward me. "The others. What are they like?"

"Like you," I whispered. "They're kind and good and lonesome. They say that they need me."

"Like me," he agreed, and the baby turned right then, rolling in a fist under my tight skin, right against Eddy Jo's hand. "And you?" he said then. "Do you need me?"

"I don't need anyone," I answered softly. Then I thought for a minute. "I chose you," I said. "It's a matter of choice."

In May I quit working at Danner's. The talk had become kind of mean around there, what with me showing, and no genuine father in sight. My men friends were happy with that, and they all said I needed to rest. I put in a garden at the end of the month, turning up grass with a hoe in back of the house by the shed, setting in snap beans and summer squash, good food, food to grow babies by. I let myself freckle, and my hair went light as I worked in the yard, and on warm afternoons I sat on the porch in Daddy's rocker, my belly all round in my lap, and I embroidered flowers and bunnies and butterflies down the front of tiny sweet wrappers. In July I painted my childhood bedroom, rolling butter-pale paint on the walls, then Jacob came out and ran wallpaper strips at the ceiling, in a pattern of bees and honeysuckle vines he'd picked out himself. Craig built a unit of shelves next to the window, including a fold-out shelf for changing the baby, which he'd thought up on his own in a fit of pride.

I grew heavy as the baby stretched out from under my breasts to my bladder, and I napped with the cats all day long, waking at noon to fix lunch certain days for Eddy Jo, going out late in Craig's truck for liver and onions at a truck stop out of town where I looked just like anybody having a baby, not necessarily unmarried. It was hard to find comfortable positions to sleep in at night, and the cats pawed around me as I tossed back the covers and propped up my legs. But the days were long and lazy, and my men friends stayed till I was sleepy enough to fall off, rubbing lotion into the swell of my stomach, then low down my back as I drifted off in the room where my parents had been man and wife, in the room where my father had died.

In the middle of August, Asia ran off. I called his name from the porch for days, Africa sitting at the bottom step, looking curiously alone without Asia. After supper, one evening, I'd sat in the rocker outside and combed out Africa' snarls, his fur shining and dense under my fingers. The moon was a perfect curved sliver by ten, and I stood on the steps and called for the cat when I felt the warm, squeezing trickle between my legs. The baby fluids seeped through my clothes as I walked back into the house and gathered my suitcase and sweater. I filled the bowls with food and water for Africa, propping the basement door open so he could get to his litter box.

I could have called my men friends, left a message with someone, maybe let them know it was time, but placing my bag in the back of the car, I decided against it. I'd call them later, ask them to look out for Asia, tell them the news of the baby. But then, under the dark sky netted with stars, as I drove out of Tyler on 301, past the diner, past the old Catholic church and Jacob's new apartments he'd bought just week, I was strong with happiness.

The labor went slowly at first, and the doctor remained at the hospital on a bed in an empty room. By morning I'd moved into the genuine throes of labor, begging the nurses for water and crying out for my mother, and once I even believed she was there. It took eighteen hours to get me into the delivery room, and in between contractions I thought of my men friends and what they were doing right then, of their eyes and their wet, gentle kissing.

We went home four days later to the house I was born in,

Alicia blinking and blind in the sunlight of Eddy Jo's car. We went home to my house, and Asia was waiting there, hungry and tired, with matted hair.

The cats liked to sun in the nursery windows, and they purred in the warm summer air as I sat rocking Alicia, her lips clenched to my thick nipples. When the baby napped, I stroked the cats in my lap, and they nosed at the front of my gown where my milk had wet the bodice. "That milk's for baby," I chided, running my fingertips down the silk of their tender throats.

IN THE evening at dusk, the men come out, one at a time, taking turns through the last weeks of summer. They bring me fresh milk and gifts for the baby—rattles, small flannel blankets, tiny socks with lace at the cuffs—the little pink gifts men pick out. We sit on the porch in the shadow of Daddy's rocker, watching the air go violet with night as the swallows scatter between the barn and the shed, while Alicia tugs at my breast. She makes the smallest noise as she suckles, and we hold our breath just to listen.

Sometimes I call for the cats, and then I bring out the brush, pulling tangles and knots from their coats so carefully they don't even feel it. Then the men hold the baby, turning her face to the last light of day, saying her name like a nursery rhyme, and look for a sign she is theirs.

CHANCES WITH JOHNSON

There's all kinds of madness in the world, that's what I tell Johnson. Some of it gets you locked up. Some of it puts you on pills so you don't have to think, just remember to breathe and eat. Most of it leaves you in the here and now, not quite broken, not quite whole.

Johnson and I talk late at night, falling off holding hands, sometimes in the middle of a thought. Before I met him, I always went to bed with the television going. I'd call for Herman and he'd pad up the stairs, slow and sleep-heavy, footsteps sounding almost human, then he'd stretch out on the rug at the foot of the bed. Sometimes the hurting washed over me so strong I'd call out his name just to hear the answering thump of his tail as it dropped against the floor.

Now I've got Johnson to talk to. I tell him, "I've been crazy, you know, really crazy." He smiles when I say this, not because it's funny, but because he knows what I've been through and he knows what I mean. Nights are the worst time for thinking, he tells me. He met me a year after my ex-husband Jim took off with our oldest son, Eddie, and Johnson says that's enough to drive anyone out of their mind. There are times I feel the edge looming up when I think about Eddie off God-knows-where with his father. It's like standing at the roar of Niagara Falls, staring down and hearing your heart say to jump. But there's my younger son, Joey, to think of, forcing me to keep one foot in the world, and Johnson helps bring me around.

We live in an old red-brick house with white shutters on the bluff looking west over Lake Michigan. Sometimes after Joey's in bed, Johnson and I walk down the narrow sandy path to the beach. In the summer you can see the lights of the tankers moving heavy and slow toward Wisconsin. On nights when the wind tapers off and the surf rolls in gently, the moon reflects in a pale yellow plate on the water. When it's calm like that, Johnson takes my hand and we wade in up to our knees. I tie my skirt in a knot at my hips and we walk where the bottom is smooth between the breakwaters. He says he loves this place. That makes me happy, because he hasn't been living up here that long, and I want him to stay.

Johnson kept on teaching high-school biology in Saginaw after his wife left, putting himself into his work so hard he won a statewide award. He's got a gold plaque from the governor, and it's hanging over our dresser. There's no question in my mind that he makes a good teacher. He likes people in general, all kinds. And he might have stayed in Saginaw forever, unhappy about the divorce, but working just to keep himself sane, except two students pulled a gun on him and stole his wallet, then hit him over the head. They charged two thousand dollars on his American Express card before they were caught. He says the part that hurts most is the boys had been students of his at one time, and he liked them. He knows all about crazy first-hand.

We both like to swim before bed when the water is warm enough, stripping down naked on our dark end of the beach, tossing bits of driftwood out into the lake for Herman to fetch. He comes pawing across the surf, prancing and growling and shaking water. Then he drops the wood at our knees in the water and we throw it back out again.

I got the dog when I moved up here with the boys, because we were all afraid in the house at night until we couldn't sleep. All those years and noise of the city behind us, and not even a thought back then as to what existed beyond the front door once the deadbolt was slid into place. There we were, all afraid in the silence of our house on the bluff, a house that grew larger in the dark, looking down on the gently lit lap of the town we'd made home. I lay awake sorting out the noises in the dark, sometimes with the boys pressed against me, and we'd whisper explanations to one another. A limb against my window. A night bird fanning down to the harbor. The buckle of a car door along the hill. The house itself, settling and creaking into sleep. We'd lived so long in the city that a big house in a small town made us jumpy, and that's what I mean about madness.

The summer nights are what Johnson likes best about living up here. We sit on the porch after supper, watching the sun as it slides into the lake, then naming stars as they appear one by one east to west. We go up to bed and pull back the covers and lie there with the breeze coming in through the windows that line one whole wall of the bedroom. The young petty officer at the

Coast Guard station said the house used to belong to a ship's captain. I say that maybe our bedroom was his, the captain's, because from the windows you can see out on the lake and down the shoreline for miles. A captain would like that. Johnson says I should think about going back to school because I have a good imagination, and people with good imaginations know how to think, and that I would do really well in all my classes. Johnson says then I could get a degree and a job. I say I like how things are, and I bring in enough money renting out rooms. Besides, I tell him, I could get a job if I wanted. I've had jobs before.

We lie there talking late, sometimes with the news playing low on the television, and we tell each other how it was before we met. There are nights this goes on a long time, because we've only been together five months. He talks about his kids and how the divorce broke him up. He tells me that he couldn't believe for the longest time his wife really left him, and how she wasn't coming back. He says that he used to be happy-go-lucky, that he could bounce back from anything. Then his ex took their kids to Tampa with her new husband, and Johnson hasn't seen them for a year and a half, which is exactly how long Eddie's been gone. And he says that his spirit's been broken. I say, "Yeah, mine too."

Sometimes he gets me to talk just a little about Eddie. I try to imagine what he's doing, and if he's still totally crazy about baseball. Johnson says boys don't outgrow things like that, especially baseball. We talk about Joey too, and Johnson says Joey doesn't like having him around. I tell him I wouldn't be too sure about that, but he says Joey feels awful because first his dad took Eddie off, and now his mother has a new boyfriend. Johnson says Joey might think I don't need him as much, and I say it's all such a mess I don't want to talk about it.

Every so often Johnson presses me too hard, asking questions about Jim and Eddie's disappearance when there aren't any answers, and I start feeling like there's a storm stuck inside of my skull. One night we were lying in bed, talking about Eddie, and he kept repeating himself, asking, "How could a father do that to a kid? How could he do that? How could he do that?" He'd go quiet for a moment, talk about something else, then he'd start up again. He kept asking, "How could he do that? How could he do that?"

"How am I supposed to know?" I finally screamed, sitting straight up in our bed. "How the hell am I supposed to know? Do I look like I know? Do I? Do I?" I hadn't known I'd start screaming like that, and I'd been surprised by the sound of my voice. The room seemed oddly silent once I'd finished, so quiet I could hear my own heartbeat drumming in my ears. Then Johnson sat up beside me when I started to cry.

"Hey," he said as he pulled me close, his jaw moving against my cheek. "I'm not the enemy." I lay there against him, crying for a while, then drifting at the edge of dreaming as he stroked my hair. We were still sitting side by side when he reached across me, switching off the bedside lamp and pulling the quilt up around our shoulders. "It's okay to get mad," he whispered at my ear, and after that I was sleeping.

Johnson and I met at a dance in the V.F.W. Hall downtown. I

didn't want to go to the dance at first, but Yubi, my friend, insisted what I needed was to get myself out of the house. She said that winter was turning me into someone she didn't know or like. Most days I spent the afternoon writing letters to Eddie with no place to send them, or calling Friend of the Court, trying to think what to do to bring Eddie back. So Yubi said, "Come on, girl, you're going," just like that. She got all dressed up in a green satin dress and matching heels, saying, "If there's only going to be one black woman at this thing, then she sure as hell is going to be one beautiful black woman," and I laughed, because Yubi's never had to worry about how she looks. Even in the morning she comes downstairs looking great, no makeup, just those big shining eyes and a smile.

She sat at my dressing table that night, twisting her head as she tried on earrings, smiling at my reflection in the mirror where I lay belly-down at the end of the bed. Watching her humming and fussing, I decided, what the hell, why sit home, and I put on black slacks and a red turtleneck sweater. "It'll be fun, just you wait," Yubi told me as we rode down the hill into town.

It was right at the end of January and snowing just a little, and we parked in a lot two blocks from the hall. Everything glowed soft and misty under the streetlights and we walked like we weren't in any kind of hurry, and Yubi went, "There's something in the air." I smiled, because there is almost always something in the air for Yubi, and she looked like some kind of beautiful angel with snow feathering all across her green coat.

We had to pay three dollars each to get inside, but Yubi said,

"It's all the beer you can drink, don't complain," as the doorman tattooed a black ink "FIRST CLASS" on our hands with a rubber stamp. Inside the hall, white crepe paper streamers hung in loops from the ceiling, and a mirrored light reflected tiny rainbows on the planks of the dance floor. Yubi knew a few women from work, and they waved and smiled at her as we walked the edge of the hall, calling out to her by name, holding up cups of beer and winking. I didn't know anyone except the chubby, redheaded teller from the bank who gave us our beer and said, "Well, isn't it nice to see some new faces coming around."

We sat at the end of a long table that was covered with white paper and sprinkled with pastel confetti. The music was loud and we couldn't talk without having to shout, so we just sat at the side of the room and drank from our styrofoam cups, but even just watching was fun. Yubi moved her head from side to side in time with the music the deejay was playing, and I tapped my feet. Since nobody asked us to dance, we danced together a couple of times. Yubi said that's how you do it, that's how you let men know you like to dance. And she was right, because pretty soon men were asking her to dance. Every once in a while, she'd check back to make sure I was okay, sweat beading up at her temples, and she'd blot at her face with a paper napkin, then go back out on the floor. And I was pretty happy just watching everybody have fun, especially Yubi, because she really loves to dance fast and knows how to move her hips so it looks just right.

I drank my beer and Yubi's beer, and I got a little drunk. Then I got more when our cups were empty. After I sat back down, a guy in jeans and a sweatshirt came up and asked me to dance. I said, "No, not to this, not fast. I'm too old for this kind of dancing," and he asked me how old I was. He looked about thirty, so I said, "Ten years too old for you," and right then a polka came on and he smiled and took my wrist, leading me out on the dance floor. We danced in two big circles on the floor, and every time Yubi's circle passed mine she'd squeal out "Elizabeth," like she was on a roller coaster ride. Then when the polka was over a slow song came on, and we danced to that. After that, I said I had to sit down and he said thanks for the dance, and that was that. Or it would have been that, except for the fact that Yubi got the car stuck when we left at midnight, and we were walking up the hill to the house when Johnson came by in his pickup and drove us home.

So that's how we met, and Johnson likes to talk about it sometimes, because he says he was miserable back then. And I guess I like to talk about it too, because I was lonely when I met him, even if I didn't realize it, even if I hadn't believed I could fall in love again, ever.

I HAVE a sink of strawberries from Lander's farm, and I'm paring out the stems to make freezer jam. It's June and the kitchen is hot. Outside the sun is white, and the sky is white, and the lake stretches out like sheet metal all the way to the horizon. From the window I watch as a steamer breasts the breakwater. I burned my back and arms picking berries yesterday, and Joey burned too, from his neck to the top of his shorts, and both of us are wearing white T-shirts today and have Nivea greased across our shoulders. I can see him from the window, his little rump sagging in the red hammock that hangs between the oak and the pole to the clothesline, and he's reading a book about volcanoes while Johnson mows the lawn. I'm worried about the grass stirring up Joey's asthma, but Johnson says ninety-nine percent of all asthma is psychological and that maybe I shouldn't worry so much. Johnson knows a lot about everything but not in a know-it-all way.

I'm standing there at the sink with a box fan on the table going full blast at my back. I've got the radio turned up loud to the Devonsport station when Johnson pulls up on the mower he borrowed from our neighbor and comes in the back door mad. He walks to the refrigerator and opens the door, stands there a minute, then pulls out the water bottle.

"Get a glass," I tell him. If I don't say that he'll drink right out of the jug. He doesn't move, he just looks at me with sweat slipping down his face and grass plastered to his calves where it flies up from the John Deere. So I pull a blue plastic tumbler from the side drainer and hand it to him. He's breathing fast and he's biting his lip, so I know something's eating at him, I just don't know what. So I say, "Johnson, what's wrong?" He just stands there, shaking his head as he drinks the cold water from the tumbler in a steady series of swallows. So I say, "Johnson, is something wrong? Did you get a letter from your kids or something?" I don't usually prod him this way. He's a talker. I don't have to prod. "Johnson?" I say.

"Jesus, Joseph, and Mary," he sighs. He's a great one for sighs. On bad days, like ex-anniversaries, he wakes up with heavy breaths and sighs all through breakfast. On bad days he goes on with his sad sighing until I grab him and rub my hands through his curly dark hair and tell him he's going to hyperventilate if he doesn't stop breathing that way. "Life's too short to go around making yourself faint-headed," I warn him.

He's standing there sighing and wiping his neck with two squares of pink-flowered paper towel. Then he says, "God damn your ex-husband, Elizabeth," and I look at him over my shoulder as I pull the drain in the sink. "This thing with Eddie is doing Joey in, you know that," and I nod my head. "He's out in the hammock, and I've been trying to talk to him. I even tried to get him to ride the mower with me, said I'd teach him to work the gears. But he says that he's worried about Eddie, and he's sitting out there watching cars go by because he thinks his dad might come back and get him too. And it stinks that he has to go through this. It really stinks."

"Johnson," I say, "I've looked for Eddie. I've gone to the police, I hired an investigator, you know that. And the court doesn't know where he is any more than we do," I say, and he frowns. Then he slams his fist against the refrigerator so Joey's magnetic letters rattle and some drop to the floor. "And I've called Jim's family and gone every place I can think of where they might be," I add softly as the last bit of sand and water sucks out of the sink. The berries spread thick over the white enamel, and I say, "It's awful, I know, but we just have to live with it for now. And I'm doing the best I can."

"I can't imagine you married to a man like that," he says, and I wince, fighting tears as I start scooping berries into the colander.

"That was a long time ago," I say, breathing deeply. "But you know what's the worst?" I add. "It's that he took Eddie and not Joey, or didn't take them both, because Joey is not as clever or slick as his brother, that's what. And he gets sick right and left. And he looks just like me, pink and blonde and fuzzy, and Eddie looks just like a real Italian, just like Jim," and now I am crying in earnest. "Parents aren't supposed to pick favorites."

I BOUGHT the house in Devonsport after Jim and I called it quits. Yubi called me in the city and told me to move on up. We'd been friends since high school, even back when black girls and white girls didn't hang around much. We'd been friends since we both lied about our ages to get jobs at the Dairy Queen on Division Street, saying we were sixteen when really we weren't. One night at closing the place got robbed by a guy with panty hose over his head who tied me and Yubi together with an extension cord in the restroom. When you're fifteen, even the bad things turn out good. Like Yubi and me. There's nothing that can come between us after spending eleven hours back to back in a dark smelly bathroom, afraid that guy would come back and kill us like he said he might.

After Jim and I broke up, Yubi said to come up and see her, to get out of the city, to clean out my heart. She'd gone up to Traverse for summer work, cherry picking, canning factories, work she said let her mind go off while she did it. Work so easy she could sing to the radio while doing it and not make any mistakes. It was Yubi's idea to settle up here like this, to buy one of the old houses in Devonsport and rent out the rooms, even if

I was only thinking about temporary things at the time. I'd lived my whole life in Grand Rapids. I'd lived my whole life in other people's houses, with my mom till she died, then with Jim in one rental house after the other, moving sideways and never really up.

I bought my own place, a three-story brick house, and it sits at the top of the town looking down over the bluffs and dunes that run along the lake. Jim and I had split up our savings and it took every penny to make the down payment, but it was worth it. The winters are cold because the place doesn't have much insulation, which is the reason we got it so cheap, but Yubi and Johnson are planning to fix that in August. And the place feels good when I walk in the door, like home should, with high ceilings, and I've stripped all the woodwork, and I've got four boarders and Johnson.

I'd been in the house almost a year, from January to November, when Jim took Eddie and and never brought him back. Yubi says Jim's a cold-hearted bastard, that he's trying to break my spirit, that he's trying to drive me crazy. I say if anyone knows how to break me, it's Jim, even if he once said he loved me more than life itself and wrote me a poem to prove it.

Sometimes at night I sit on the bed and stare at myself in the mirror. I try to see what's different, what's changed, what's there now that wasn't there with Jim. He said I was the one who changed, after all, not him, but I only see who I am. Me. Elizabeth. I don't really think Jim's trying to hold onto the past, at least not how it was when we were married. I think he's trying to teach me a lesson, and he thinks he can do that with Eddie, and it's rotten how he's hurt Joey in doing it.

He blamed me for the divorce, saying if I'd never taken that job at the V.A. hospital that our life wouldn't have gotten so messed up. Something happened to me when I took that job, and that's what I can't see when I look in the mirror, trying to figure it out. The closest I can come to explaining it, is that the world inside that place was more real than the world outside. I was an attendant, so I really got to work with the men there, and I realized how you can't predict what life will give you, even if you plan. I'd be with those guys all day, spooning in food to someone who didn't know me from Adam, changing diapers, or shuffling cards for the ones without hands. There were old guys there, guys from World War II, and ones from Korea, Nam, stroke victims, guys with plates in their heads, quadriplegics, guys with kids, guys that used to have the world by the balls. Eight hours a day I'd love those men who'd been dumped off there to die. I'd go home to Jim and the kids after work and get scared, start thinking how nothing lasts forever, everything is just for now, how there is no promise of life ever being what you expected. Jim said I should quit because he was tired of coming home to a woman all tied up in knots over nothing. He said, "Over nothing." That killed me. But I couldn't quit. I needed what I got from those guys, needed it like a fix, because it made me so full, and Jim couldn't do that.

Maybe that is a little thing to break up a marriage over. I don't know. I just know I needed Jim to wake up and see that life is something new each day, to look at his kids and say, "Jesus, I made these kids with Elizabeth," to say, "The sun came up this morning and isn't that pretty great?" But Jim was going to be the best production manager at Keebler, ever. He was going to whip his crew into shape and change their attitudes. He went off to work at six every morning and came home at seven or eight in the evening. His clothes smelled like cinnamon and nutmeg and almonds. The scent never washed off his skin.

One night he came home and I was crying because Don D'Ambrosio died on my shift. The boys were watching television, and I was trying to fix goulash, but every other second I was crying and trying not to. I was trying to believe that Don really was better off dead, because he'd been so unhappy lying in bed and not really living like he did before half his belly got blown away. Jim came in and took one look at me and said, "What the hell's going on here?" and I told him about Don, how I was holding his hand when he died. Then he told me to get hold of myself, because the boys shouldn't see me so upset.

"I am upset," I told him. "And maybe the boys should see me like this. Maybe they should realize that life is not all one big party. Maybe they should see that things get a little rough sometimes."

"They're going to think something is wrong here," Jim said.

"Well," I said. "You know what? Something is."

JOHNSON COMES over to the kitchen sink and stands behind me. He places his wide hands on my shoulders and spreads his fingers, pressing gently against my T-shirt and sunburn. "Elizabeth," he says softly, and I turn, leaning into him hard and quick. "God, I wish I could help you," he says. "I go around here fixing things up, but the one thing you need most, I can't give you. Do you want to get another lawyer?" he asks as I cry against the sweaty, damp warmth of his chest. "Yubi says we could hire a different investigator."

I twist then and look through the window to the yard. Joey is standing near the edge of the road, kicking in the dust so it rises in a cloud at his ankles. I've paid three different agencies to track Jim down, but they've all trailed just a step behind him. They can tell me where he's been, not where he is at this minute.

Johnson feels me looking out the window, and he turns just enough to see Joey lift his hand to his eyes and rub. "I wish I could help him," he adds, and I start to cry harder, choking against Johnson's chest.

We're standing there when Yubi comes up from the basement. She's humming some church song under her breath, and we don't move apart when she walks into the kitchen. She goes, "Oops," teasing, like maybe she's caught us kissing, then she sees I'm upset. "What's going on here?" she says, and puts her hands at the flare of her hips. She stands there looking at us with the wicker laundry basket overflowing at her feet, and she says, "What's the problem, Baby Bets?" I'm her Baby Bets, white, tightest friend.

Johnson shakes his head. "Elizabeth is just having a hard time. We were talking about Eddie and how Jim took him off."

"Girl," she says, and whistles through her teeth, "that is enough to make anybody cry. Cry a river, if you ask me, Baby Bets. Lord," she says as she turns, carrying the laundry down the hall to the den, and we hear her going on. "That Jim is nothing but a cold, ugly, nasty S.O.B., I'm telling you, God ain't done with him yet, no sir, he's going to have to do some kind of praying to save his white ass when they catch him." Then the television comes on loud with soap opera music, and she closes the door, and it's quiet again.

Johnson and I just stand there a while, and after a bit I quit my crying, shuddering down inside his arms. I pull away from him then, from the lawn mower scent of his chest, and I smile. I look at his face and rub a smudge of motor oil from his chin. He's been crying too. "You miss your kids, don't you?" I say, and he nods. "Aren't we a pair?" I laugh gently, and he closes one eye, then he opens both of them wide, green eyes with thick, black lashes.

"That we are," he says, and he pulls me against him, so close I can hear his heart.

JIM AND I fought about sex. He said what I needed was to go see a shrink, because after Joey came along, I didn't enjoy things so much. It hadn't always been like that. Once upon a time, I couldn't wait for him to get home from baking cookies to jump into bed with me. Once upon a time, in another world, I'd stick Eddie down for a nap at lunch, and Jim would race in for a quickie. It was just that after Joey arrived, things changed. There was laundry and diapers and feedings and flu shots and ear-aches to deal with. And Joey's delivery itself was a nightmare.

I went home from the hospital with my belly all flabby and a sunken, sore half-moon where they'd finally had to reach in and save Joey. I couldn't nurse him like I did with Eddie, because I was sick the second time after losing so much blood. Then the incision got infected, and my bladder prolapsed. So there I was, carrying around a baby who was all gassed up on formula and crying, my bladder leaking into my panties, and Jim grouching out loud that I was just about as fun as a corpse. Life isn't always fun, I told him.

A few months of living in the middle of all that, and I decided on my own to get help. As I dialed through the list of family counselors in the phone book, the hardest part was explaining the exact kind of help I thought I needed. Even once I figured out what I had was marital problems, I hadn't been prepared for being placed on a waiting list. I left my name with half a dozen clinics and got referred to several others, and not one with any opening sooner than two months away. Then just when I'd given up believing that I'd ever find help, Dr. Lois Harper left a message at work for me to call her.

In the middle of my afternoon break, Dr. Harper took my call as I stood there at the pay phone in the hospital lobby. "Elizabeth," she greeted me. Her voice was throaty and warm, and not what I'd expected. "I got your name through Family Central, and I have an opening tomorrow evening if you'd like to come in." It was as simple as driving downtown after work. It was as simple as saying I'd be there.

From our very first session in her third-floor office, I knew Dr. Harper was exactly what I needed. She was a large, round woman, fleshy all over, and with a great shelf of breasts that rested on her belly. While she appeared over forty, that might have meant fifty or sixty, but I couldn't quite guess, as her face was pale and plumply softened. She filled the door to her office side to side, and had a big head of bouncing red curls and blue eyes. I'd expected to meet someone in a gray skirt and jacket, perhaps topped with a white cotton lab coat, and I got Dr. Harper in a lavender jump suit tied off with a paisley sash. I'd expected a woman wearing horn-rimmed glasses and sensible shoes, and I got purple velvet slippers and burgundy nails. I'd expected something else, but I found what I needed. I found someone who laughed as much as she listened.

Dr. Harper's laughter surprised me at first, as I'd been hurting inside for so long. The first week we sat there face to face in matching blue recliners, rocking forward and back until I'd gone through the list of my problems at home. "And?" she smiled brightly when I seemed to finish up.

"And?" I echoed back, then I paused. "And I think I'm going crazy, that's what," I cried, and she lay back in her chair and started laughing out loud.

"I'd feel crazy, too," she announced. "I'd feel absolutely mad," she smiled. "It's okay to feel crazy." Then she rocked forward and handed me a box of blue tissues, staring straight into my eyes as I blew my nose. "And there are ways to make things better," she promised in a whisper.

Dr. Harper's laughter let me learn I could turn crazy into something else. Between listening and laughing, I started to believe there were all kinds of chances for things to work out, and that life could be a balance of both pain and hope. I learned that I could take responsibility for enjoying sex, if I wanted to,

but that was the part Jim didn't get. The part about wanting to.
I went alone to my appointments at first, then Jim started going
with me when we kept having problems in bed. That was Dr.
Harper's suggestion, but mostly Jim just liked to tell her what
was wrong with me, and how nothing was wrong with him. She
suggested ways to help me to learn to relax and explained how
he could ease up a bit. But Jim never'd been easy before that,
and he kept on hovering over me, rubbing me so hard that I felt
like I was being erased. I was tired, and my heart turned away.
So I faked it, moaned out some version of ecstasy, and of course
I felt guilty and horrible. And sad.

I talked to Yubi about it. I had to tell someone. She said she'd
probably fake it too, if she were me. "Absolutely, Baby Bets."
Then she added, "And if I was afraid of losing my man." And she
said, "Are you?"

"Am I what?" I said.

"Afraid of losing him?" she smiled.

"No," I sighed, and I meant it. "You know what I want Yubi? I
want a little tenderness, a little patience, just a little. That's all,"
I said.

"Girl, don't we all," she said. "Don't we all."

JOHNSON'S THIRTY-THREE and I'm forty-one, and I tell him I like
the difference. He says my age makes me more stable, more
compassionate. More grounded, he tells me.

"Than young girls with smooth skin?" I ask him, and he
blushes.

"That's not what I mean," he says. I tell him there are a lot of us around. "No," he says. "Not like you. See," he explains, "you weren't looking for somebody."

He likes to throw off the covers at night and look at me naked, run his fingertips over my nipples and trace my scar with his lips. I get embarrassed, tell him not to look so close or he'll get scared, but a part of me likes it. His ex is an aerobic dance instructor with black hair cut close to her head. Sometimes I think about that when we're in bed, think that I might not measure up. But, Johnson's so patient those thoughts don't stay around for long.

Johnson's got wide shoulders, but he's a little flabby. Not much, but not perfect either. And when we're in bed I don't forget how I look, but it just doesn't matter so much any more, because I am just me and Johnson is just Johnson, and it's all that we got. And sometimes when we're done, I lie there and smile and he goes, "A penny for your thoughts," or something silly like that.

So, I tell him, I go, "You know what's so great is that this is so ordinary. So lovely and ordinary," and he smiles. It's the closest I get to talking about love.

IN AUGUST I tell Johnson I will give him the money if he wants to fly his kids up for a visit. "No," he says. "But, thank you for offering. Maybe at Christmas."

We're on the third floor, putting in a shower and a stool so there'll be a john up there for the boarders. It was Johnson's idea to fix up a bathroom for them. He says it'll be more private that way, that the two floors we live on will be our own then. So I go, "Hey, if it's the money that's keeping you from saying yes, please take it. I have enough from the rent."

"No," he says. "Besides, I think Joey is getting used to having me to himself." Then he says, "I got a job in September."

"You're kidding," I say. "No one gets work up here out of season."

"I did," he smiles. "I'm going to fill in at the high school for a woman who is out on maternity leave. I'll teach biology and earth science."

"You said you didn't want to teach if you didn't have to," I say. "You said Saginaw ruined you on that, especially high school."

"I said that?"

"Yes. You said that last spring."

"Well," he says. "A lot has happened since then. Right?" he says. "Right?" He frowns for a moment as he tightens the shower head, then shouts, "Watch out," and turns on the water. "It works!" he cries in genuine surprise, which surprises me back. I think he's a genius. He pulls me inside of the fiberglass stall, then he kisses me under the water. When I close my eyes, it feels just like rain.

JOEY IS ten, and he's always had asthma in the fall, every year, no fail. But this year it isn't so bad, and the doctor says being on the lake helps. And Johnson has allergies, so the two of them come home from school and take their medication and hang out together. Sometimes they work in the yard, or they watch television together on the couch. Joey tells Johnson things he never tells me, and I'm surprised at the things I hear secondhand. Johnson's right about Joey thinking his father doesn't love him, but he doesn't push him to talk about it. And I don't think he's trying to replace Jim. Not really. I think he's trying to be a friend.

In September, when everyone is gone during the day, I get a little itchy thinking about Eddie. Now that cherry-canning season is over, Yubi got hired on at the lumber store as a cashier. I don't have her to talk to, and the boarders all work daytime jobs. So it's just me in the house thinking about things and painting the front hallway and freezing vegetables in zip-lock bags and labeling them.

And then late one Friday afternoon the phone rings, and it's Eddie. I can hardly believe it, because I'm always thinking about him, but when I hear his voice on the phone I can't figure out what to do. He goes, "Mom, I want to come home. I miss you and Joey."

So I get my voice real level, because I am about in tears, and I say, "You can come home any time you want. Just tell me where you are."

"I'm in Grand Rapids with Dad. We've been here six months, but he said you knew I was here," he sniffles. "Dad said you wanted me here because I needed to spend time with him, and that with Joey getting sick all the time, that two boys were too much trouble for you," and then he is crying and trying to catch his breath.

I'm mad as hell at his father, but I try to sound calm. "Listen, honey, your father didn't tell you the truth. I've always wanted you here, and I've never stopped wanting you here, ever, and I mean that. Just tell me where you're living, and I'll come and get you."

"Dad'll kill me," he says.

"Eddie," I cry out then, "your dad broke the law when he took you away." My voice is shaking. "I can't come and get you unless you tell me where you are," I explain.

"3149 Westphalia," he answers. "But I think we're moving."

"Why?" I say. "Why?"

"Dad is packing all our things again," he says, then he starts crying again. "Mom," he says in a quiet little voice, "come get me."

"Don't worry," I tell him, trying to reassure him, even though my heart is breaking up in my chest. "You just hold on, because I'll be there."

By the time Johnson's car is coming up the hill, I'm wild and running out the door. I'm still telling him about the phone call as we drive out of town. Joey is sitting in back, and he's asking a million questions and I tell him to just take it easy, that nobody knows what will happen. But we're too late, because by the time we get to the address on Westphalia, the sun is setting, and Eddie and Jim are gone. We go to the houses in the neighborhood and ask people if they know Eddie or Jim, but they don't. And I can't believe Jim's been with Eddie in Grand Rapids all this time, almost on the street we once lived on as a family, and I can't believe they are gone, and nothing Johnson can say will stop me from crying. Nothing.

THE NEXT couple months I'm really low, and I tell Johnson I feel like I've gone past the bottom and I'm hanging in space. I spend my days calling long-distance directory assistance in Michigan cities and asking for listings under Jim's name, but without any luck. He's vanished again, and I can't pass a minute without thinking about Eddie. Half the time I can't eat, and when I do I throw up. Johnson's good with Joey, taking him roller skating and to play putt-putt golf in town. I go from feeling helpless about Eddie, then to feeling bad about how Joey's stuck in the middle of this mess. More than anything at this point, even with Johnson to take up the slack, Joey's my son, and he needs to believe that I won't let him down, but I'm in a slump and I can't get out.

One day we go into town to eat at the inn and there's a family there with six kids, and the mother, a skinny redhead, keeps saying their names, and they all start with *K*. She goes, "Kerry, stop that. Kim, let go of Kyle. Kelly, wipe your face. Krissy, Kevin, sit up and eat." I sit there and watch them and my food gets cold, and I can't stop watching them. Johnson takes me home and puts me to bed and sticks a thermometer under my tongue and a heating pad at my feet. He says I need to see a doctor. I say I will. But most of all I need to see Eddie, and I feel like I could kill his father. I could. If only I had the chance.

SO I go to the doctor and find out I'm pregnant. I guess I knew all along. But I can't make up my mind to tell Johnson. I can't decide if I really want to be a mother again at my age, and with things like they are. And just when I decide I could love a new baby if I had one, that maybe it would be the best thing, I find a note from Johnson on the edge of my dresser. He tells me he'll be gone for a while, and to please, please not worry. And it's signed, "Love, Johnson."

YUBI SAYS Johnson really has gone to see his kids because the school says that too. In the note he said he'd be back, all that kind of stuff, but I don't believe it and I don't care. The doctor says I'm almost three months along, but it's not really a baby to me, not in my head. Not like it was with the boys when I wanted a family so bad, even if Jim and I fought. So at three full months, I'll make up my mind, decide if I'll have it. I tell Yubi I got a bun in the oven, and she says it's a sign, and I say she's crazy. I don't believe in mystical junk like that. All I know is there is this little knot growing inside me, and I should have told Johnson I loved him.

IT'S THE middle of November, and it still hasn't snowed, and Johnson's been gone three weeks. I tell Yubi I think he cut out. She says she doesn't think so, Johnson's not that kind of guy. I say what does she know, maybe he got back with his ex-wife aerobic dance instructor with the sleek body. Yubi says not to think like that. I tell her I can if I want. She says go ahead, nobody's stopping me.

So I wake up on a Thursday, the day I told Yubi I'd decide about the baby. If Johnson had come back. Yubi says to make up my mind for myself, because the one thing that should be important is what I think.

AROUND NOON, I put on my coat and red rubber boots and walk down the beach to the breakwater. All the kids are in school, and the summer people have left, and the dunes are empty. The wind's blowing sideways, flattening the tufts of grass that cling to the sand. Both foghorns are sounding, first one then the other, echoing back and forth between the lighthouse at the end of the pier and the Coast Guard tower on shore. The water is rolling in so hard I can barely make out the wailing of the seagulls hovering over me, and each time a wave hits the breakwater it bursts into spray. I stand at the end of the pier for a while and think about what I should do, listening to the call and response of the foghorns.

Mostly I'm thinking about chances with Johnson, about chances for happiness, the chance for this baby, the chance that I'll end up alone again. I stand there at the end of the pier and I make up my mind. I'm going to have this baby. I will have this baby because I miss Eddie, and Joey needs a family, and because I think Johnson is long gone. And in the end I know I've made the right decision, even if it was a hard one, even if I had to make it alone.

THE NEXT morning I take the old bread and rolls from the kitchen and climb down the hill to the lake. It rained all night long, and the day is thick with mist. The gulls hover and cling in a swooping circle as I toss up crusts and crumbs. I'm walking back up the hill to the house, thinking about how I'll tell Yubi I'm keeping the baby, when I see Joey coming around back by the porch. His yellow rain slicker is sailing behind him, and I start to run toward him, holding my arms out. And then I have to stop for a minute. My breath is short from climbing, and I can already feel the baby pressing against my bladder.

I'm standing there holding my side and thinking about making French toast for breakfast, when another boy rounds the house, taller than Joey, dark, and yelling, and I know in a flash that it's Eddie.

There's no stopping me then. I'm racing over the wet grass, slipping in the mud by the garden as Eddie rushes against me. I'm holding him then, so tight and hard that he squeals, lifting him up until his legs wrap around my waist.

I've got Eddie at my shoulder by the garden when Yubi comes around the corner of the house, shouting and picking her way barefoot across the backyard. Her hair's still up on her head in red plastic rollers, and she's shouting and laughing. She's laughing and hollering out, "Baby Bets, hold on." She's hollering my name, and right behind her is Johnson, with Eddie's suitcase in his hand.